The Shimmer of the Assistant

And Other Tales

The Shimmer
of the Assistant
And Other Tales

Hermann Stehr

K A Nitz
LOWER HUTT

Der Schimmer des Assistenten
first published 1914,
Der letzte Akt first published 1913,
Die Großmutter first published 1914
and
Der Geist des Vaters first published 1917

These translations by Kerry Nitz
Copyright © K A Nitz 2013
All rights reserved

ISBN: 978-0-473-24249-7

National Library of New Zealand Cataloguing-
in-Publication Data

Stehr, Hermann, 1864-1940.
The shimmer of the assistant and other tales /
Hermann Stehr ; translated by Kerry Nitz.
ISBN 978-0-473-24249-7 (pbk.)—ISBN 978-
0-473-24250-3 (online)
I. Title. II. Nitz, K. A. (Kerry Alistair), 1971-
833.91—dc 23

Contents

The Shimmer
of the Assistant

1

After the assistant, Paul Förster, had spent a month in anxiously impassioned consideration of whether he was fulfilling the hopes which beset him from the eyes of his fiance and from the blessed base of his own soul alike, he tried to show some resolve.

He drafted a request for a higher salary and bore it personally to the offices of the directors.

And now he was standing in the office of the director of the "God's Blessing Mine" and looking with extreme tenseness at the director's face leaning deep over the large, densely written sheet. The assistant battled against fear and servility, which made him feel ashamed because he knew that it would startle him when the director straightened up and looked at him. In order to bear up in a manly way, he turned with an inaudible step to the long, yellow table which, littered with maps, payrolls and records, took up the entire centre of the large, cold room. He leaned on its edge and assumed a casual pose. For it was ridiculous, as a thirty year old, he could not behave like a young clerk, even if at the present time it was perhaps better not to stress independence and dignity too much.

Then the director lifted up his fat head of thick white hair, pushed the sheet away slightly with his hand on the writing desk, stroked his grey moustache thoughtfully and said with good-natured regret,

"An accursed tale, my dear Förster."

"Yes, Mr Scheithauer ... Director," the latter corrected himself, moved away from the table and returned to his old subordinate pose.

"A very inconvenient time," the director continued, "the administration is contented with you. But they cannot initiate anything with their benevolence during the present miserable economic situation. You know that yourself. One cottage after the other is putting their fire out. The railroad is electrifying. The textile people are suffocating on their inventory. We are only operating with half the work force. For heaven's sake, we even have to hold tight to every pfennig."

Scheithauer had worked his way up from clerk to director and did not yet rattle his tongue lieutenant-like, in order to preserve his authority, as was now generally becoming a bad habit in Prussia, but behaved graciously and courteously to everyone.

The good, decent man had paused and was waiting for an answer,

"You know, director, I have been with the administration for eight years and believe I have a claim for that reason," Förster said with a wavering voice.

"If it came down to just you and me, certainly. But if we give you a raise then Schirsager will come after you, Mayer ditto, and before we could catch our breath, we would have to promote the lot of the entire suite of clerks."

"I wasn't meaning a promotion, director ..."

"I know. You are only calling for a salary corresponding to your seniority."

Förster paled and just nodded.

Scheithauer rose hastily and paced a few times back and forth with large strides by the long table.

"It is only twenty marks a month more, director ... and they would, I think, suffice for the present," Förster said pleadingly.

Scheithauer interrupted his wandering with a jolt and returned to the writing desk, emitting an impish whistle.

"Haha ... so, so, hmhm, you think so? Ah now I understand! You want to marry."

"Now yes, director, I am thirty. You know, I lost my father and mother early, you get sick of living at the inn and, well, in a word, it isn't to be ashamed of that you yearn after your own home."

There was a long pause. The director raised his brow in thought and looked out the window at the thick, white vapour streaming past which the wind was driving across from the coking plant. The machines sniffed wheezily like heavily laden horses being whipped up a mountain.

"Yes, my dear Förster," Scheithauer came out of his solitary musing again, "that isn't much to want."

"I have been getting a hundred and ten a month for four years," Förster said quickly and anxiously to preempt a negative reply.

"Well ... need it be then?" the director asked and narrowed an eye impishly.

"How do you mean, director?"

"Ah ... haha! ... I mean, if you are forced ... you know, we are all sinners."

"Absolutely not, what are you thinking?"

"So, my dear, if you haven't broken a leg — now I'll speak as your older friend, not as your superior — then I would advise you still to wait before founding a family. No extra pay can be given. Impossible, quite impossible! Well, and what more do you have then? You will not be well-fed by love, and you manage comfortably now with your salary."

"Comfortably ...?"

"Well, yes, nobody can just make leaps, my dear, not even I."

Paul Förster now looked out the window at the hulking wooden cooling tower. It was gagging in his throat, the brown stained tower swayed in the mist. For a moment, the fury boiled up in him, 'Dammit, keep the money, it'll work out the same.'

But it did not get any further.

Director Scheithauer saw the expression of dogged energy on his office assistant's face and said,

"Of course I don't want to stop you from marrying, on the contrary, the king needs soldiers. Certainly. I even want to befriend you. You will receive a larger dwelling, a patch of garden will be found, the coal allowance will be increased. So, why shouldn't it work out?"

The assistant, Förster, stood stiffly with a pale, desperate face and strove bravely to smile affably.

He would have liked to have made one last attempt to induce the director to at least an extra pay of ten marks a month, but it seemed impossible for him to bring any words forth. For he would then have become uncouth and — have been lain out on the street on the next "first".

"Now think everything over again, dear Förster, and let me know your decision in fourteen days so that the necessary steps can be taken," the director said with a sympathetic voice.

The assistant made an awkward bow in agitation, murmured some senseless phrase with an abject voice and stepped with a secret curse of fury through the door and into the hallway.

Paul Förster had, one time in his childhood, as a boy of twelve or thirteen years, he did not know exactly, seen through the window from the supper table at which he sat together with his father and mother a not overly distant mountain slope. The last cottages, the little church and above them the narrow, dark stripe of forest; everything lay in a gentle, white light, in such a blissful unreality that he had been as happily shaken in his soul as by nothing since in his life. This picture hung unblurred in the treasure house of his memory and had over the years gradually become the measure of all the pleasant strokes of fate which befell him. And if some beauty that he met on the way was suffused by a light that faded the brightness of that early child-hood enlightenment for him, then he wanted to hold that for the greatest happiness of his life, to comprehend it in enjoyment modestly and with nothing contrary to it. He had planned to do that and had waited all the time since the early deaths of his parents, through all the pinched loneliness of a poor orphan, over the pitiful clerk's appren-ticeship, until he was finally at a point to be able to keep the minutes himself and possess his own desk in the office, at which he alone was master.

But always, if something had outshone in its expectation the shimmer of the picture in his soul so that he thought he had attained it, so that he then wanted to be content, if ever such a thing had carried him away far over his hopes, the disappointment coughed all the brilliance from his eyes. For as soon as his yearning had materialised, it faded and the light of that remembered image had not, as he had probably thought, been made homelike on his earth by reality, but shone more alluringly and remote as ever.

While Förster strode down the long corridor of the mine administration building and slowly came down the short, stone stairway to the lower floor, he considered everything and came to the conviction that if he did not make the marriage a reality now then he would have to wait his whole life long in vain and have in the end nothing but this fantasy image in his soul.

So as not to excite the mockery and schadenfreude of the other clerks, he stepped quietly into his office, put on the protective sleeves of black smocking and continued on the fair copy of the hearing over a mine explosion in Erlicht, Plot 49b, Land Register 256, Volume III.

He spent the evening at home and filled it again, only more passionately than usual, with deliberations and analyses of how, despite the failure of his hopes for a raise in salary, the maintenance of a modest household could be made possible. He surveyed his clothes and established that with great care he would not have need of a new acquisition for three years. His bachelor's furniture would suffice as furnishing for the living room. Then it only remained to acquire the kitchen and bedroom furniture, for which the five hundred marks saved by his girl, his Mathilde, even if not quite sufficient, would have to be used.

He had taken the path to this point so often that there was no stone to kick which he had not turned twenty times, no attempt which he had not made countless times, no twist whose odd anxiety he had not, who knows how often, over-come in the end. But heretofore he had always been able to save himself in the hope of a raise in his salary, by which he had been put in the position of concluding every procession of worries with a brandishing of the flag of future plans.

Now this short indulgence in a distant, varie-gated air had been nailed up for him, and with a fearful energy, he set about the reconfiguration of his entire way of life. For since it was certain that his future household must be defrayed with a monthly income of 110 marks, all the calculated security of existence had collapsed into itself.

Paul Förster sat down and divided 110 marks in a tyrannical, almost insidious manner, shuf-fled items when nothing more was left, pinched five pfennigs from each meal, observed every dish minutely, looked in the pot every day, worked out the influence of the seasons on his calculations, ransacked the rubbish bin and lost all control after hours of self-torment: invented income and divided it by months, weeks and days, calculated the daily expenditure of every married official and did not rest before he had brought their existence into distress. In the end, he could not continue and it seemed to him as if he had strolled about a strange city at night, quite senselessly and pointlessly, had called like a fool into every open house door and now went exhausted into the blankness without knowing where a roof over his head or a bed for the night was to be found.

Then it struck twelve from the tower of St Mary's church. He stood up, extinguished the lamp and stepped to the window, exhausted, fearful almost to tears, leant his forehead on the cold glass and implanted in his mind the firm decision, against all these mountains of obstructions, to keep the word he had given his girl. Only it was already more like living the courage of a man who, churned by rushing waters carrying him away, sees all prospect of rescue vanish.

The short lane at the end of which he lived was stamped full of the black night, soundless, walled up by darkness. Fancifully distant outside, a pitifully red veil of light wavered, turning paler with every flicker and yet not able to go out.

"And when we marry," the assistant said, "our poverty will begin and all the deprivations of our childhoods from which we fled. With every bit of bread there is fear, every thread must be reeled off from the heart and every dress must be cut from the body. — Mathilde, don't you see it?"

He called as though for help, with exhausted, failing voice.

In this moment, a gust of wind rose in the neighbouring street and travelled blustering and rattling past like a long train of galloping goods wagons.

Förster breathed out relieved, fled his narrow room and ran on the rough pavement towards the red veil of light which flickered in the darkness of the broad street. Just as he stepped out of the narrow lane, a new wind gust raged. The barber's bowls whirred like castanets, signboards swung on their hooks, house doors creaked, the electric tram's wires swished.

The assistant was enshrouded and pursued by the noise. And while he was carried away thus by the turbulence, the long restrained fury boiled up high over his downtrodden, powerless life.

"Miserable gang! ... That a man should sell his happiness for your money ... thrown in his face ... like a knave ... a man has to take your office."

With a pale face, he screamed out his indignation to the entire town. It was all the same to him, they could all be lounging in the windows.

The clerk risked everything: in the darkness, in the middle of the night wind's noise, all alone.

The few revellers who saw him gesticulating took him for a comical drinker and glanced at him smiling. So Paul Förster strode along the streets out of the town and sank onto a bench in the park which consisted of a few trees.

2

After this night, the assistant was ruled for days by a state like that which at moments physically plagues a man who has had the wind knocked out of him. He lived between two breaths and did not find the courage nor the strength for anything. He met the director with downcast eyes, and he thought of his girl with averted trembling. Yet he did not turn away from her, but stared in her direction with a clouded-over look, enfolded in shadows. He waited thus for the light around her to go out, that radiance from himself which her image raised into an unreal blissful brightness.

He did not go out for three days, but lay the entire time, often even in the work hours, under a hidden lurking force. It was in vain. His thoughts were like a hand which was grasping after something in a large, dark barrel.

On the fourth evening, Paul Förster reflected that it was necessary for her to be "informed of the altered state of affairs" and to find out "whether her intention nevertheless remains as before".

He knew that she left the shop in which she was a salesgirl at eight o'clock, but he did not start on the way to her house until an hour later, and then a quarter hour later, carefully pressed in the shadows of the row of houses opposite, let the agreed upon whistle ring out in the twilight of the narrow, deserted street. The light in her window went out immediately. With that he was smitten by a fright, no, a cold fever. He abandoned his place hastily without really knowing why and stepped five houses deeper up the lane, under a dark archway. — Hardly had he found himself there than he heard the familiar creaking of her front door, and straight after her steps pattered down the footpath, shortened, came up to his hiding-place, hesitated, beat a retreat hastily, as though breathing out, and then oscillated for a long time abidingly back and forth.

"If she truly loves me, her heart must find me," he said to himself. Thus a quarter hour passed. Finally he heard her steps tailing off towards the main street. He ducked out from the gateway. Then he stepped onto the footpath and saw how her slim figure disappeared upright and hasty in the garish light of the bustling street. Her blond hair was blazing white at the temples.

"She doesn't really love me," the assistant said to himself and took a few slowly weighted steps towards her, but soon desisted from that and, after aimless wandering through a series of half-dark side streets, walked into a familiar tavern. The landlord was leaning by the oven corner and his fat face smiled half-drunk. The two front rooms were almost empty. In the back room, a loud party was raving. Förster sat down and ordered a glass of beer.

When he raised his face, a young man of about eighteen years was sitting at the table opposite him. He was narrow chested, very pale and sickly; but his eyes were exceptionally large, beautiful and full of a smouldering, melancholy fire. He looked ever lost in himself as if he was alone in the room. As soon as he felt Förster's eyes on himself, he became self-conscious, lowered his head and began cleaning his nails. That happened a few times. In the adjoining room meanwhile, the noise was increasing. Drunken men's voices were beginning to sing, shrill women's voices whirled in accompaniment. They flirted with a few standards. Suddenly everyone exploded into whinnying unanimity and sang,

"You've seduced my woman, you've seduced my woman."

Förster saw the young man turning even paler, pausing with his hand before his eyes for a moment, then standing up and stepping behind the curtain by the window. Nothing protruded but the left hand holding the curtain back. It was bloodless, thin, as agonisingly despairing as no face Förster had ever seen before. As if thereby the young, pale man was crying out painfully.

"Perhaps he loves one of the women," the assistant thought and in the same moment saw his girl's slim figure disappearing upright and hasty in the garish light of the bustling street.

In his soul up to now, it had been faltering, dark, perplexed. Now somewhere, he could not see where to, a door of salvation sprung open. Once more he touched with a glance the youth's despairing hand. Then something of its shaking and indignant shock sank into him. He put down the money, left the beer half-empty and slinked hurriedly past the sleeping landlord out of the tavern.

So it is with cowardly, weak and discouraged souls.

When the assistant, Förster, got up the following morning, he had the feeling that his girl had deceived him.

Murky, but at the same time it was as certain a the fact of his birth. It had happened, only he did not know how, did not want to know either.

For a few days, he did not dare at all to follow that scent with his thoughts. In the mist, as he saw himself over his own shoulder standing at the window and staring out into the night of the street; with one hand, he held the curtain pulled back. The grasp of his fingers lay shaking, painfully around the folds of the material. Trembling and bitterness over his feelings poured through his arm. For he had run into the streets nightly because of her and waited on her for hours in vain and she? — She? — went and sank into the red exultation of delight.

From existential cowardice, the assistant, Förster, fled completely into the temper of the strange youth that he had met in the barroom, and acquired by a covert theft of the soul everything that he needed for the execution of his intention. This intention alone too, he bore unconsciously in himself like stomach acid.

He felt the deeply despairing look of disappointment in his eyes as it had shimmered over the face of that pale, young man. His stride became stiff and hesitant, like the gait of that stranger. At every opportunity, he let a heavy sigh climb into his chest. The image of this stranger rampaged through his inner being like a dream of a white horse.

But his own soul made itself quite small, held back all movements of its peculiar being and cowered motionless like a mouse scared to death in a dark corner of his breast, more a pulsating point, a shaking drop, became a being with an ability to see which it suppressed, an ability to ponder which it expelled, a gift of memory which it shunned. Quite far off, borne by the wind, not by mundane circumstances, the tender sounds of hours of love wafted, the magic of mutual hopes, unrealisable pictures of intoxicated eyes, in brief, the follies of love which are made more blessed than all the deepest ideas of wisdom.

The concatenation and confusion of dread by which the assistant, pushed aside by this beauty, had been taken into a strange type of captivity, felt to him like the incomprehensible, undeserved coincidences of an adverse fate. Regrettably, wrongly deceived, Paul Förster had come thus far in the eight days since his interview with the director, and when a colleague, who had his desk in the same room, askew next to the door, after some intentionally eye-catching looks mentioned his completely altered behaviour, the assistant lowered his eyes, blanched from the stranger's soul outwards, felt driven from the office and, for probably more than half an hour in the middle of his workday, sat on an old heap behind the pit and lost himself in the distance with the melancholy of another vista.

We all do not know how often we have been driven into that strange state, and perhaps it is really an everlasting trick of scared, weak souls to escape responsibility in difficult life situations by such a confusion of their inner existence.

The confirmation of his complete alteration by his colleagues imparted the assistant's situation with the irreversible. Where everything previously only wavered around him like a self-generated dream, now Paul Förster felt wedged between the immovable walls of a fate and began automatically to act dispassionately.

The Saturday held both hands to its cheerful mouth and ran with the blasts and shrills of the factory whistles through all the lanes. The workers streamed out the gates afterwards, swung the blue enamel coffee flasks in their hands and laughed to the pleasures of Sunday, whose shimmer breathed all kinds of motley promises in the grey air of the smoky lanes.

On the way home, the assistant drafted in his thoughts the letter which he wanted to write to his girl. "Dear Mathilde! By the displacement of the business and all kinds of unforeseen reversals in the economic situation of our branch, I did not come all week to visit you until the evening on which I waited in vain for you. You probably have other appointments, with which I do not want to be in your way. A genuine love, however, is like a good copy: it agrees in every way. So that we can finally make ourselves clear to each other, I suggest a walk through the Steinau forest tomorrow afternoon. There we can speak, and finally, if God wills it, we'll stop off at the registry. I will expect you at three o'clock in the afternoon at St Mary's church."

It all ran effortlessly in his head as though drilled on a secret parade ground in his thought.

Without any appreciable change, he put the sentences down on paper with his pleasing penmanship and was only beset by a certain distress because of the closing. "Your loving Paul" was too affectionate; "Your Paul" too hard.

No, neither worked. From too much love, it came badly to that end which he had in mind, and with rasher hardness, he took on the suspicion of a certain purposiveness. But it was only necessary to let the actual circumstances speak.

After some new changes which he found and had to discard again, he broke off the manly striding over the short floor of his room and stepped to the window, out of which a part of the serpentine lane in which the assistant lived could be overseen. Between two houses of the row opposite, he also had a limited view of the "God's Blessing Mine" in whose offices he "worked in the Department of Mine Affairs," as he expressed himself. You saw the tall chimney straightaway and to the left and right of it a part of the coking plant. There, behind it, a grey confusion of old rooves was jumbled altogether.

The snoring of the conveyors, the rattling of the wheel works, the growling bluster as if from the centre of the earth, the wind shredded, ravished clouds of steam from the smouldering outcast mass of coke: it all produced in the assistant the sense of a great personal meaning and thrust the awkward interview which was in store for him tomorrow in the Steinau forest into the region of undeserving, painful affairs. Why must it happen to him just now? To him, who had never before done the least wrong in his employment?

Without knowing it, his body flowed into the gestures of the youth who had captivated and abducted him days before: his upper body huddled into itself and became so bent over that his right hand grasped clenching into the folds of the curtains and the opposing leg had to brace itself post-like on the floor to prevent the clerk from collapsing.

Thus his body's stolen gestures lay entirely in the bitterness of an undeservedly hard fate. He remained in this distress for a while, then stepped to the table and wrote under the finished letter, "Your painfully afflicted Paul."

After he had put the letter in the next post, he dawdled through the rest-day-animated darkness of the factory town like one digressing in denatured idleness, from whom unfavourable fortunes have struck every pleasant object from the hands, every stout-hearted plan from the head and every bright hope from the heart. He lay awake for a long time and looked up into the empty, morose, confused whirl of the night.

3

This sickly fog into which he had pushed himself imprisoned the assistant without light even after rising, he even pursued his inner life cautiously so as not to tear the redemptive cloud.

Rochlitz, as the factory town in which Paul Förster lived was called, had quickly arisen from a small colony, as quick as a rubbish heap collected from the refuse of the surrounding houses. Wide stretches of land contributed so that the bluster of its dogged industry, the fever of its lustful greed, the miasma of its stinking breath and the puffing of its shafts, the coughing snores of an incurable illness could remain.

The town ate like a festering, giant scab further and further into the serpentine valley, and, even in the night, a hum sounded around it as though it was sending out an army of sleeping drinkers who were still being racked by hallucinations in their befuddled dreams.

That was the usual state in which Rochlitz kept itself. On some days, however, it broke out into a true delirium. Then it sucked the storm from the air and did not rest until it was roaring through the streets so that the clouds of unswept dust veiled the blocks of houses. Men rushed in it as though in flight, the electric tram tinkled despairingly and sped groaning from it, and it whistled over the rooves and clapped through the heights like the swish of corded whips.

Rochlitz had just embraced such an outbreak of desperation over its existence on the Sunday on which Paul Förster was waiting for Mathilde by St Mary's church. All the excrement of the place was dancing through the air. The assistant pressed himself into a corner of the red brick building. The gutters sighed above him, the tower clattered softly with its wooden blind in the uproar, and sometimes it hummed weakly as if the bells themselves were being disturbed in their timber housing. Paul Förster leant in dull melancholy against the wall, held with his cane onto his straw hat, cursed quietly from time to time over the awful weather and then surveyed the small square which was like a narrow funnel in which the swirling wind continually stirred everything like crazy. As if every electric tram brought a new charge of wind, the bluster rose stronger again and again and the people were turned into red, green, blue shreds of clothing by the circling clouds of dust. For a while, everyone screamed confusedly, the bells rang like shrill distress signals, and in the next moment, men were rushing in search of their hats rolling past the assistant, and women and children, one hand on their hat, the other holding their dress down, were being pushed laughing by the wind.

"I will not place myself in the dirt," Paul Förster said each time a troop of people blew past. He looked over more keenly and, when he had noticed nothing but unfamiliar people, sunk again into his melancholic protective rapture.

Then he all at once caught sight of her blue dress and coloured-leather jacket.

He walked over.

The moment that he reached her, the girl turned around and looked back sharply through the yellow whirl of the short lane to the church square.

"Who are you looking for then?" he asked sullenly behind her back. She turned around lightning quick at the sound of his voice and said pouting, "Well, but Paul!", but could not speak further for young men's voices were howling in the square in comical desperation, "Mathilde! Miss Mathilde! Where have you put yourself?"

The girl smiled and said without looking,

"They're the two from the clothing shop next door and young Janus."

"Who's this Janus?" Förster asked dully, but to himself so that the girl only heard him grumbling.

Mathilde strafed his motionless, melting face with a glance.

It was impossible that she could have acknowledged his unfriendliness any differently, for the three quickly struggled over swinging their canes with humorous heroism, the first a fat, stocky plug, the second a delicately airy banner, the third lanky and swaying as though bound together from nothing but laths.

He was the sworn jester and sang with crowing voice,

"Rochlitz is a swine's slit."

The others laughed at it in the overloud merriment of fellows on the loose.

Paul Förster took his hat off dolorously and attempted an austerely formal introduction in the tumult,

"Paul Förster, assistant to the constr..."

But the lanky Janus did not let him finish, saying instead exuberantly, "Not needed! Not needed! We'll do the same with breath and without dust. Come, children!"

Thus the three trotted on laughing and Paul Förster walked sheepishly next to Mathilde behind them.

The young people's voices spun continuously, and one after the other they looked around with impish smiles at the silent couple, in suppressed mockery as it appeared to the clerk.

Finally he said, "This doesn't suit me. I'm turning back." But he said it so cautiously again that Mathilde understood nothing, and when she asked him what was up, he smiled painfully his dolorous smile, but continued to grouch in silence that the men had no education, were immature clappers and that it was not the company for him. An interminable, smouldering cloud steamed from him. He walked with lowered head in it without throwing a glance at Mathilde, and yet with a painful satisfaction, he felt the delicate movements of the slim, blond girl next to him, heard her soft step and felt the clenched breath of her unease. But his soul, perceiving all that, this pitifully pulsing point, this hidden little mouse, twitched confined in a secluded corner of his breast and was not permitted to be brought to light by the grey vapour of the strange being.

He let out a heavy sigh.

Mathilde turned her head startled, and because his face nevertheless remained lowered, she touched his arm and whispered to him, "Dear Paul, pull yourself together as long as they are with us. They are just laughing at us."

"You don't know how I suffer," he replied depressed, "but you are right, one must have courage."

They had come by a few side streets out of the dispersed, small houses of suburbia and were now striding along a dirt road which rose gently up a hill towards a not overly distant forest, striding more and more out of the region of the riotous dust cloud. You could probably still hear its rumbling rebellion in the tall houses and see it then filling up the whole place with the billows of its yellow fumes wailing, but you would be disturbed by nothing more than fine grains of sand sometimes being driven in your face by scrambling wind gusts.

The young people now stopped for a moment and looked gleefully at the grimy tumult behind them.

"Cheers to the meal," Janus said and dried the sweat from his hat with a handkerchief, "God has drummed and whistled so that we don't have to go in the dirt carriage down there anymore," and without signalling he turned suddenly to Förster, "Don't you think so, mister assistant? — Now, by the way, the solemn moment is here: Albert Janus, brain plasterer, that is bookseller, these two men, Ohme and Zingler, figure people out respectably and deceive them respectably, that is they make men's clothing: and I do you the honour of knowing you by renown, you are Mr Förster, am I right? The 'God's Blessing' of Miss Mathilde Schreiber."

Perhaps the nonsense of his chatter would have gone away in a while, but he was hindered from that by his friends in cheerfully crude palpability. Between the three, a jesting duel arose which segued into a race.

They trotted off jubilantly like boys playing.

Almost at the forest, they turned around, brandished their hats, shouted "adieu" with panting laughter, and Janus crowed from a distance through the funnel formed by his hands, "We leave you to your ease — but please, if it is done — is do o o ne — best without hope — withooout —"

Then they sprung into the forest and began singing the "Silesian Song".

The assistant had wanted to involve himself in the introductions, but had not managed it when faced with the verbosity of the bookseller. For that reason, he now walked more depressed than before next to the girl.

"Listen," she said after an apprehensive spell, obviously in an endeavour to start a conversation.

The song of the three was quickly drawing deeper into the forest as if it was being sucked in by the greenery, and in the end it was ever so soft and indistinct to the ear, like a melodic seething of the needles.

"No? Beautiful, Paul, isn't it?" she asked devotedly and looked him fondly in the eyes. "Shame on you, not once have you offered me a good day!"

Förster scratched in the grass self-consciously with his cane, then pulled himself together with a sigh, looked straight in her face as though to make a scathing accusal, but let his tense breath out again dejectedly and said in denial, "No, in the forest, come ..." Then he struck out along the path with quick strides; his gait soon became a hurried run.

The girl followed him breathlessly.

"Just what is it then?" she called after him, "don't run so! I can't keep up. Paul! — What's gotten into you!"

Deep in the forest, he finally stopped. His eyes were blazing. With tempestuous breath, he waited impatiently for her.

But before she had reached him, he broke free, "... Yes, just come here. — Always come here. Don't just feign it. — Yes. — Do I believe that it's hard for you. Haha."

The girl stopped white as chalk, as though rooted to the spot.

"Paul, dear Paul!" she said reproachfully and grievously.

"That's right. That's right," he bowed towards her and threw his hands out at the same time, scornful and inviting. "Please, step closer! I have a good conscience. I'm not in awe of myself. But it must come to an end. That's right, to an end. It's no use, no use, no use."

The poor girl moved towards him under the hail of words, sat down on a tree stump and said coolly, "Now say what happened." Then, listening, she covered her face with her propped up hands.

The assistant hesitated and, astonished and confused, measured the calmly and submissively seated girl. But he took a hold of himself and began walking back and forth with quick, snorting strides because he did not know immediately whether he should continue blustering.

"Now just speak," Mathilde reminded him calmly and looked at him enquiringly.

"Do you want to ridicule me some more?"

"I don't think so!"

"Now, then, why are you speaking like that? I have a post. Even if it is small, it is secure however. We'd get through, for sure, even if everything is more expensive, pork ninety, beets a mark. I know all that. But I have no fear, none at all, haha!"

"Well — and?" the girl asked raptly.

"Yes — — and ... and ... For certainty there must be love."

"Your Mathilde has no love?"

"No, at least not the right love."

"And why?"

"Because ... because ..." The assistant saw that his girl was earthly pale, expiring, with pounding bosom, waiting on his words, and his confined, ill-treated soul was urging him to fall on her, to embrace her and, asking for forgiveness, to bury his hammering head in her lap.

"Because?" the girl asked calmly, since Förster had fallen silent stutteringly and was staring at her lost with large eyes.

"Because the faith is missing ... the faith," he finally put forth falteringly, startled at the same time to the core by a soft, infinitely high, blissful singing tone which rang out still deeper than in his breast, swung in him for a while and then tore apart shrilly, so shrilly that the feeling came over the assistant that he was lifeless.

At the same time, the tree trunks around him shook as though from an invisible blow, and then, as the inexplicable, soundless shivering quickly subsided, lost the mysterious brilliance of their lonely beauty and stood like dead, senselessly painted planks. Their rustling whined like grit rolling over a sieve. The birds droned like tin pipes.

The assistant looked around anxiously and did not comprehend what had happened.

"I have to sit down," he murmured feebly, slowly pulled himself together like a marionette and took a seat on the ground opposite his beloved, pulling up a leg, laying his hands clasped together on it and staring at them in dull rigidity.

He offered the sight of a despairing man.

The tears were running over the girl's pale face.

"... And how do you know that I have become unfaithful to you?" she finally asked quietly, gently.

Förster just nodded silently and then propped his head in his hands.

"Paul, at least speak," she urged him, trembling.

The assistant emitted the groan of the other, closed his eyes like him and began monotonously to speak with a quite strange voice, "I was walking about in the night, up and down the streets. For you don't have any peace when your trust is gone. In the storms, you know, then I sat and waited, but you did not come before my eyes as usual. Rather a man whom I didn't know. And when he could come instead of you, he must be closer to you than I am. Do you see, do you see."

Then he sank down again into dull silence.

"Paul, you're ill. For sure, as I can't think how you could otherwise think of such conceits. Look at me. As if I could deceive you," she said and tried to rise to step over to him. But he stretched out his hand dismissively and shook his head.

"No, no," he continued speaking downcast, "I know everything. You see, I went to the director for a salary raise. I have done everything as we had agreed upon. Everything. And if we also had to save, a lot, to the utmost, yes. For the ... the ... hound! ... the gang: they sent me away ... That is, I'm still an assistant ... oh yes. You see, but nevertheless they added not a pfennig, I'm stuck."

Mathilde had trouble following the confused words of her beloved. But with a woman's instinct, she surmised the context and swayed her head reproachfully.

"I would not have thought that of you," she said sorrowfully. "But you know I'm not like the other girls here who only think of clothes and treats. You know me, that I am used to being at home saving. So, you need have no fear of this unfaithfulness. That's what you mean, isn't it, Paul? Please be honest."

The assistant emitted a nasty laugh in answer.

"Oh, you women," he then said hostilely. "Do you think I don't see through everything? That's right, I learnt it from him, I tell you, and he knows about it, but thoroughly! He heard them singing, my friend? Do you understand. And they are all the same."

Mathilde now rose troubled and looked pondering at the ground for a moment.

"Hm. And who is the man that has told these lies about me?" she asked tensely. "I want to know."

Förster just shook his head and stared at the ground.

"Nothing. Nothing. Ha!"

Then he raised his face. It was painfully pale like that of someone dangerously ill, and his eyes had lost all expression.

"You heard me whistling in the evening? You see, I had come then to tell you everything. I, dumbo, stand and wait and wait and stand. While you walk up and down feigning as if you are looking for me. But I know, you don't *want* to find me. And then you go to the other man with whom you arranged to meet on the main street. I saw you flying down the dark lane into the light. To one of the nasty ones who sing, who sing those damned songs that make you want to tear the curtains from the window."

Now Paul Förster was in the middle of the other man's indignation, jumped up shaking, stepped over to the girl and screamed in her face, "That's right, so it is, so it is!"

But instead of being shattered, the girl abruptly began laughing merrily. —

"You dumb, jealous, dear boy. Paul, now just give me a kiss."

She threw her parasol to the side, embraced him passionately and pushed her face to his.

But the clerk broke free and pushed her away so that she staggered.

"Get away," he screamed, "get away! It is over, completely. Go your own way, I'll go mine, it is finished. Over. Over."

He screamed discordantly, hoarsely, like a despondent convict, and trembled like someone who has committed a crime under the power of another and could no longer find his way out of the entangled whirl which the stranger had befogged him with.

Then the clever girl did not understand the lost man either anymore and saw herself driven by his brutality from their world into a confused darkness.

She thought she had been displaced from the heart of her beloved by the love of a rich woman and took his mad ferocity for the consequence of his bad conscience.

But all that was forced on her at this moment by the feeling of sorrow, shame and humiliation.

She threw one more glance at Förster, who stood there obdurately and stared into the berries in dogged paleness, picked up her parasol and said with unnatural calm, "So, so. — Well, I wish you more happiness then with your richer woman."

Then she went away with careful steps over the hill.

When the light of the field blossomed into the darkness through the dispersed trees of the forest, she abandoned her composure, she sobbed loudly and plunged fleeing into the open air.

4

Paul Förster did not have the courage to look up at her. He riveted his eyes' tense look on an ant at his feet, which was endeavouring to get a grain of sand between its pincers in order to carry it away. It kept slipping away from it, it kept tackling it again, each time wilder and wilder, more dogged, more obstinate. It planted its feet so firmly in the ground that he thought he heard it. The sound of the steps with which Mathilde stole from the forest sounded to him from the insect's course.

"How such a small creature behaves," the assistant said.

Mathilde's steps rang softer and softer and more and more distant.

"It doesn't stop going," Förster pondered.

Now the girl cried out muffled, and then it was suddenly so agonising, so apprehensively quiet everywhere, as if the entire world had been struck dead.

The ant at his feet rose up on its hind legs and cleaned its pincers.

The assistant was seized by fear and rage. He clenched his teeth and jabbed at the insect with the point of his cane.

"You don't want to bellow so, you lit — tle — sod, you ...?"

He pulverised the ant into mush, and while he drilled the cane with both hands up to the ferrule in the sand, his body was convulsed from head to toe by the cold horror of fear, because he knew that he had killed an innocent creature. But his anguish cooled into new cruelty and his ferocity into new repentance.

He laid the weight of his body on the hook and did not stop forcing the cane persistently into the earth.

His breath groaned and tears were running over his face.

Suddenly the cane shattered, the assistant tumbled backwards and fell to the ground.

"Oha," he said laughing out loud. "I will yet break my nose. Ola! Ola! Hahahahaha..."

He scrabbled up laughing and sat down on a tree stump.

But during this whole mad merriment, the tears were running thicker and thicker over his cheeks.

And when he now saw his shattered cane, the fright took away the anguish for a moment. He walked around appalled, stared in the direction in which Mathilde had gone away, slapped his hands over his face and broke out into loud crying.

After the first passionate eruption, the sobbing merged into a moderate outpouring, but it could not be stopped until the last drops had been pressed from the assistant. Finally, pumped dry and staggering, it seemed to him that he was awaking from a turbid, wild dream, of which nothing more remained but a weak, powerless humming which suffused him.

His soul, which during the eight-day odyssey of his inner being had been cowering, travelling as a blind passenger in a dark corner of his breast, had lost itself entirely in its depths.

Paul Förster rose from the tree stump on which he had been sitting, and stepped over to the half of the cane which he had bored into the earth. He did not succeed in recalling why he had done it. When he infiltrated into his thoughts, he only came as far as the empty humming which suffused him. He looked at the other half of the cane in his hand to get some clarity, but found no trace there either to lead him back to it. The day was passing away. The trunks were already sway-ing uncertainly in the darkness, and when strands of mist drew through the forest, it seem-ed to him as if the trees were being lifted up and tumbling deeper into the shadows of the night.

All around the deer were also starting to draw in to graze. The silence was suffused everywhere with the soft, mysterious rustling of small steps, all approaching the assistant.

Then it started getting eerie for the clerk. He threw the remains of his cane away and began fumbling his way haphazardly from trunk to trunk. When he felt a path under his feet, he made quicker progress and soon stood on the edge of the forest. Down below he saw Rochlitz. It had had its fling and was crawling through the night quietly and tortuously in the shimmer of its countless lights. Like a giant worm, covered with glittering scales, soaked in precious life, the place lay burrowed in the pool of the dark night, sometimes snoring leisurely and sated from the sunday-quiet pit, and blinked bluishly lustful now and then with the lights of the electric tram into the smoky blackness. Thus Rochlitz rolled on and did not move from its place.

Paul Förster was frightened as though by a desolately threatening hallucination which he had never seen before. He crept back into the forest and reached from tree to tree deeper into the darkness. In the emptiness of his inner being, a vague certainty that somewhere there was a quiet, blissful shimmer he had once possessed sometimes flickered up. He staggered through the black silence of the forest after this gentle bright speck in the world, soon losing all direction, stumbled over steep slopes, sprang over creeks, crawled up precipitous walls, and called out constantly, "I am the assistant Paul Förster! I am the assistant Paul Förster!"

Woodcutters found him in the morning lying seemingly lifeless on a path up the black mountain.

He was taken home and the summoned miners' guild doctor diagnosed a severe nervous breakdown.

For weeks his condition alternated between raving and deathlike silence. When he lay in that mute state with extremely lucid, large eyes, it looked as if he was awake and looking over all the world's secret interconnections.

Once during such a time, Mathilde Schreiber visited him, impelled by the conviction that she had wrongly imputed to him as a moral affair the brutality of that break in the forest, because he was certainly already in those ill-fated hours disoriented by the gathering fever of the illness, as if a driving against her will had fallen from her. Yes, the good girl went so far in her pity as to see the great, painful torment which had obviously befallen the assistant because of her as evidence of the strong lovesickness which bound him to her.

She approached his bed and looked in shock for a while at first into the faded, almost frozen blue of his eerily motionless eyes. Then she wanted, with a voice stifled by emotion and painful love, to express all the love of her pitying heart, but got no further than the greeting and a few exclamations, for the old despair was suddenly thrown into the face of the patient and the next moment, the raving thrust again through all the contortions of his body and soul. The girl was led out by force and the summoned doctor explained that with the end of the delirium either his life would come to an end or with a favourable outcome a lasting mental derangement would set in. Everyone, even the doctor, was wishing that the former would occur. For that reason, they took notice of the inefficacy of the sedatives with concealed gratification. It really seemed that everything in this body was being smashed into debris. The assistant's every breath was fluttering out, tearing the last sound from his throat, shredding his heartbeat, and in the end, it was as if someone was treading on his chest.

Then he lay in agony. His lips lost their colour. His eyes rolled back. He lay cold and stiff. His face was covered and the door was closed to begin the preparations for the burial the next morning.

But when the woman came in the morning to wash the corpse, the face towel lay on the ground and the dead man asked with barely audible voice for a drink.

After fourteen days, he left his bed.

A month later, he was again sitting in the administration building of the "God's Blessing Mine", assiduously bent over the files which had been brought into serious disarray by his stand-in, and worked with such devotion as if his illness had been nothing but a lengthy gathering of his professional powers. All digressions into addictions, every touch of a dreamlike mood, the variegated glance, the excess shimmer of temper, it had all been obliterated from the assistant, the memories of his love had been extinguished with the shadow of its shadow.

Mathilde Schreiber waited in vain for him to return to her.

Finally she took heart and went to him one evening. He was sitting on the sofa and leafing through official documents which he had taken home. When she entered, he raised his head and asked her in a polite business voice to take a seat.

Without an emotion entering his face, he listened to her regret at misunderstanding him that time in the forest. Without coming to her aid, he could see how the girl struggled in shame and confusion to hint at her loyalty, and even then he still remained calmly patient as she sat there with flooding eyes, speechless over so much insensibility, and waiting for at least a kind word of farewell.

His lips remained closed, his head inclined attentively, and because she continually fell silent, he invited her with a reminding glance to continue and made a few impatient writing motions on the paper with the dry quill.

Then the embarrassed girl pulled herself together and said, rising, with a barely audible voice,

"I'll return to my parents in their little house and help them in the cultivation of their strip of field, turning the soil, harvesting, tending the goats, and think that I would have been better not to have come here. For I've lost everything that I brought with me to Rochlitz." Then she left him a moment's time for an answer.

But he rose, laid the quill down like someone pondering, said, "Yes, yes, that would be best," and watched indifferently as she backed away out of the circle of light from the lamp and slipped silently through the door.

That night the assistant slept somewhat uneasily and the next morning, he was tormented by a vague anxiety that he had forgotten to make an essential report to the director. It concerned the disclosure that he had refrained from his intention to marry.

But he could not think about it anymore, he constantly felt a weak clenching in the region of his stomach, a soft pressure on his neck and had the painful feeling of a dereliction of duty.

Towards eleven o'clock, he heard the steps of the director in the hallway above.

Then his unease increased in strength so that he stood up and went up to the director's office, for he entertained the hope that the forgotten thing would occur to him if he stood opposite the director.

But on entering the room, only a deep despondency befell him. He sat on the proffered chair, looked tensely at the floor and then asked with a timorous voice, one would probably come away empty-handed with it, if recently a mistake had happened now and then. He felt again quite well and was happy in his work, but the aftereffects of his illness were still a little in force.

The goodness and the comforting encouragement of the director forced the tears of emotion into his eyes, and he returned to his desk more together and certain.

But for his whole life, he remained afflicted. After every completed work, he did not cast off the apprehensiveness of having made a crude mistake. No amount of diligence, no amount of attentiveness freed him from it. No amount of praise could reassure him entirely. He was named superintendent of his department and finally mine administrator. But he received all the honours with the melancholy of a concealed embarrassment. His step became scuffling, groping. He only ever spoke in an apologetic tone, greeted people as if caught, could only sleep by naked light and avoided walking alone on secluded paths across the fields or in the forest because he always heard someone creeping behind him.

The Last Act

The usual company were sitting with the regulars in the White Bear: the bank manager Klöhn, the engineer Wiest, the valuer Klose, the schoolmaster Doctor Wickel and the master builder Schliemann.

The vaulted, browned premises were empty and an almost dejected mood reigned at the round table.

"Landlord, Rosenkavalier!" the fat bank manager cried with his rich, asthmatic voice.

"Better let it be, Klöhn, he's dragging even more today. You know how sensitive the temper of his leg is with a loss of takings. He drags it then so that it appears on the stage a good five minutes later than its master," the youthful Doctor Wickel said and stroked his coquettish little moustache up at the corners of his mouth.

"Hoho, that you can see," the entire corona cried in the next moment, for the hotelier waltzed his fat body through the doorway smiling. It was a cheerful sight for the carousing society as Mr Bittner entered lightly and hopping.

"He's cheating!" a few cried; others commanded, "One, two! One, two! Lift the legs!"

Bittner headed for the boisterous sea, stepped up to the bank manager and asked elegantly, "And you'd like, Mr Bank Manager?"

"Customers," Klöhn said and opened his large eyes even more, "a double helping of customers, Mr Landlord. The beer tastes like the premises, completely empty."

"If everyone was doubled, then doubled three times as Mr Bank Manager calls for, then nobody would need come in anymore," Bittner parried wittily. Everyone knew he tended to be a bit of a joker.

"In what way?" master builder Schliemann asked and rubbed the blue ridge of his nose cheerfully.

"Master Builder, don't push, let the man speak alone, for he has the rhetorical agoraphobia. Take care, he stutters already with his eyes," Klöhn's voice sprang crowing in between.

The hotelier paid no attention to him, instead he turned to Schliemann and said, "In what way? Well, because then I would have 35 men here."

Engineer Wiest, a lanky, thin man with a large square-built yellow face and a black mongol's beard under an enormous hook nose, had sat there until now as if asleep. Now he straightened up, shook his head and said to the landlord, "In what way. Schliemann means in what way is the man on the bench doubled three-times?" He was already speaking somewhat awkwardly.

Klöhn sprang up excitedly, "I have ..."

But they did not let him continue, "Sit down, Karl, you weren't asked," they all shouted at him.

When it was quiet, Bittner answered,

"Because Mr Manager shouted for six, Mr Schliemann."

Klöhn, "I have to as well, for you are deaf for three."

Bittner, "Not even on a leg, Klöhn."

Wiest, "But the thing doesn't tally."

Bittner, "Why, Mr Wiest!"

Wiest, "Well simply because six times five is thirty."

Bittner, "Certainly, but if you are right then the gentlemen don't count for anyone. Six times five is admittedly thirty and the table with five in place makes 35. My calculation differs from your's only in that I don't treat those present as nothing. I give my regards, gentlemen! If you need anything again, I am gladly at your service."

With that the hotelier left the company which was working itself up. The five men fell amongst each other and after a while, the noise of a considerable, festive market arose.

But strange. After barely ten minutes, the same taciturnity had sucked every word from their mouths again, and they laughed at each other mockingly and shifted their glasses.

Only the engineer Wiest sat there again as though asleep. The master builder, who had kept his place next to him, touched him now on the shoulder and said, "At least tell us the story,

Wiest, which you were prevented from telling us yesterday."

"It won't work today either," the schoolmaster whinnied cheerfully. "As thirteen is an unlucky number and he has already had his thirteenth."

The engineer raised his head slowly and directed his small, sharp eyes at Doctor Wickel. A bitter expression lay in his unattractive face. He eyeballed the schoolmaster sharply. Then he asked scornfully, "Do you know why I drink more from time to time?"

Someone made a sign to the schoolmaster not to give a sharp answer, because they knew that the engineer was in a phase in which his temper sometimes seized him unexpectedly.

For that reason, Doctor Wickel answered softly, "Because you sometimes just have more of a thirst."

"So? Do you also believe, like all beasts, that you drink with the stomach, young animal tamer? Haha," Wiest said and shoved his glass onto the table. "Most people drink with the brain. That is, those who have one which is worth speaking of ... and you must have regions in it ... all sorts of regions. Then you go somewhere else with every drink and the more you drink, deeper and deeper within yourself. In the end to the point of creation."

"Well, well, that was where you broke off yesterday," the master builder said, when Wiest had lapsed into taciturnity again, sitting there with outstretched long arms and fixating on the table top.

"For God's sake, Schliemann," Klöhn spoke beseechingly,

> "but you know it; barren becomes the soul, when it is sweetened by alcohol."

It was familiar to everyone that between the bank director and the engineer, a secret enmity had existed since ten years ago. At that time, Wiest had lost 30,000 marks on a security which Klöhn had given him advice on, no, directly urged, a few said. The bank director maintained in contrast that Wiest had been obstinately emphatic about the transaction and so was himself at fault for his loss. It had not come to a legal dispute between them. Both treated the matter more like an unpleasant bagatelle and agreed on the form of a reciprocal behaviour which often even led superficial observers to the belief that between the two men there existed, despite the difference in age — Wiest was forty, Klöhn was sniffing deep into the fifties — there existed an affectionately pert relationship.

Nitpickers and moralistic point scorers admittedly inferred from this over-ready forgivingness of the pair a deep divisiveness which balked at the light. Both Klöhn's daughters had in particular had at the time the short but brilliant blossoming of their youth, so that for months all married and unmarried enthusiasts for love had been seized by rapture and flung at their feet. In the midst of these outrageous triumphs, "the most beautiful sisters", as they were called, disappeared on a journey whose progress and goal remained veiled in darkness. During their half-year absence, the rumour spread that both girls were addicted to perverted desires; and, as though in confirmation of this slanderous murmur, when the "most beautiful sisters" surfaced again, they were hardly to be recognised. Really, they looked like wrecked priestesses of professional love and even the magic of youth had disappeared from their voices. Their admirers drew back from them as though from a blow to the forehead. The engineer Wiest turned strange from about then.

He provided his service at the ironworks as usual, but took on an ever-smiling face, a mask-like, almost idiotic smile and a constantly wisecracking cheerfulness from which he was freed to a sleep-like state in weeks of days-long alcoholism.

What proceeded in the man's soul during this period of inebriation remained a puzzle to everyone. But if someone wanted to throng him with questions during it then he became furious, and once he had even torn all the glasses from the table and smashed them on the wall. They respected this oddity in him because Wiest otherwise abounded in cheerful thoughts and wordplay and was a harmless, good fellow. The relationship to Klöhn remained amicable over all the years, if both also occasionally rubbed against each other.

Since half a year ago now, the engineer's "intermissions" had ensued in ever shorter intervals. It was forcing something out of him, for every time he tailed off in inebriation into turbid intimations, arrayed absurd ambiguous assertions or quibbled about the beginning of stories whose telling, however, he never came to. Instead, he suddenly turned pale with fear, rose shaking and went away with withdrawn head.

Klöhn suffered under this change in Wiest as though under the reproach of a heavy debt and punctiliously aimed at bringing the engineer to an explosion. For this reason as well, he repeated today the mocking verse, declaiming laughing,

"but you know it; barren becomes the soul,
when it is sweetened by alcohol."

The engineer let his arms lie like two batons on the table, laboriously raised his head a hand's breadth again, then inclined his right ear to- wards the table and said, almost slurring, "Now listen, gentlemen, listen, wood fibres are like the cells of a body. The deepest life pecks in them, the life after death."

Doctor Wickel looked at the valuer indignantly and said softly, "The thing is hopelessly dreary today. Will you leave with me? I'm off."

The two pretended to seek out the toilets, made it into the hall without attracting attention and disappeared. When the master builder saw that the two were not coming back, he suggested to the bank manager that it would be best to leave Wiest to sleep in peace and to leave as well. Klöhn shook his head energetically at the offer of Schliemann, shrugged his shoulders and looked around in a sort of turbid, aggressive obstinacy at the premises which were still empty, barring two lovers who had crept in soundlessly and were now sitting there wordlessly and sinking over the edge of the held-up newspaper with enraptured eyes into each other's soul.

"Because of those two," Klöhn thought scornfully, "and if there's no change, we'll move him into the back room and onto the sofa."

Schliemann also went away silently and waved from out the door with his hat. He made a face at the same time, which adjured the bank manager to treat Wiest quite carefully.

Klöhn relieved his mind with gestures. But when he heard the door softly shutting, he rose with the grotesque frog-like hastiness peculiar to him in order to run after the bolter. For he wanted to inform the master builder that he held it as his duty to not desert the engineer, in order thereby to allay the suspicion once and for all that he was still secretly afflicted by Wiest. That was not the case. But it provided the bank manager with the pleasure of reaching the door to the premises, through the hall, looking cheerfully for the vanished master builder and then returning to the table as though to a good deed. He found the engineer in a quite altered attitude: upright, pulled up, his arms crossed over his chest.

"Well then, engineer," Klöhn said, sitting down with intricate waving, "that is excellent! Cheers!"

Wiest made no reply, but looked tensely at the table as if he was counting with his eyes.

The banker observed him for a while from the side and found that the engineer was perfectly switched on again right up to the automatic movements of his pupils.

"A funny dog," he then said to himself, "oh well, I'm shooting off. For once I have to get into the open air."

He talked out loud to the engineer as follows, "The constant isolation doesn't do one any good."

Wiest remained silent, nodded his head and continued the motions of his pupils. Then Klöhn afflicted him further. "God stop me. I don't meddle in the affairs of others. But it appears to me, you are slipping in this regard too."

Wiest's lips remained shut.

"Obviously it's not something pleasant which comes over you from time to time," Klöhn continued his pressing further.

The engineers mouth shook as if he was biting an inflamed toothache.

"Bank man," he then said softly and mysteriously, "moderate your voice ... voice ... a little. — Better that you just whisper."

"Well, what we have to say, everyone can hear," Klöhn replied. "Even the couple — who are sitting by the fire," he added carefully.

Wiest looked over at the lovers — extremely conspicuously and for a long time. Then he returned with a deep breath again to his incomprehensible absorption, shook his head, inclined his upper body forward and said so softly that the banker did not understand it, "You know nothing of the gravity of spiritual sensualism, bank man, nothing of that spiritual conjuncture, and that it belongs to every person, for example, that it is capable of persisting in us as perception of their appearance longer than their presence; and for that reason men can also linger longer in one place than their body, than their own spiritual conjuncture of course ..."

Klöhn looked at him amply and thoughtfully.

"I have nothing against philosophy," he then said, "but everything has its bounds. You have to kill off such things. I can't endure them without schnaps."

Exasperated, he blew his breath out and called loudly, "Two Dornkaats. And quick."

The engineer's pupils were moving again. He sat stiffly and looked at a point. The boy brought the schnaps. The engineer tapped with his little finger as if listening to himself, tipped the glass onto his tongue and then continued,

"You see, bank, hmhm, bank ... damn it again ... the lamps aren't burning! — So we'll let that be. Men linger longer than they are there. For example, Klose is still to be perceived softly. Look, Klöhn."

The bank manager thought, "Curse it, I'll endure it." He looked in the direction indicated.

"See, the others are the weaker personalities. They have already disappeared. But Klöhn, look, Klöhn ... pardon, Klose of course ... look, now he is also beginning to fade. Do you see it, bank man?"

"Certainly, of course, yes!" the bank manager answered eagerly, though of course he had not apprehended the slightest.

"Adieu, Mr Klose!" The engineer bowed to the empty chair and then stroked his right hand over his face. His fingers were contorted as though cramping and trembled as if freezing.

"Ah, you know, Wiest, we should quit that topic. It's uninteresting, by God, absolutely," Klöhn said.

"Klöhn ... you are Klöhn, though, aren't you?"

The engineer reached across uncertainly, groped a few times next to the bank manager's arm, but then caught hold of it and pressed his lower arm warmly.

"Be at ease, it will be equally interesting for both of us, especially for you, I think, hahaha!" Wiest broke out into loud laughter and hammered his fist on the table at the same time.

But he suddenly stopped laughing, became pale with fear as usual before finishing, pulled his head down into his shoulders and examined the bank manager with rigid eyes and motionless face for a long time. At the same time, he moved closer to him along the bench and suddenly said hoarsely, "You have something on your neck, permit me to say."

"What? Kindly leave it be, Mr Wiest!" Klöhn sprang up and sat down on the bench.

"What was it?" he then asked smiling to smother the fright which he had been beset with by Wiest's sinister approach.

"A black beetle, that's all," Wiest answered, at once quite broken down, hanging sunken over the table, his eyes extinguished and speaking to himself almost inaudibly, "... that's all ... it was running around on you for a long time ... Then I couldn't help it."

"What?" Klöhn asked, it was beginning to get sinister for him.

"But you ... but you ... that's right!" Wiest cried out without paying attention to Klöhn's words. His cry sounded desperate.

Down the hall, the barman could be heard coming. Klöhn seemed stunned, turned with an apologetic gesture to the lovers and hurried out to hold back the service; the engineer was off his rocker again, and while he was saying that, the landlord also came and laid his hand on Klöhn's shoulder enquiringly. For that reason, the bank manager said the remainder to the hotelier without interruption, "Yes, you know, Wiest has the boozing poison. I have, as it were, got his hackles up and must now see to dealing with him."

"Perhaps I should sit with you," Bittner interrupted him. "Come, we'll give him change for his big notes." With that the hotelier turned towards the door. But Klöhn primly pulled him back,

"For God's sake, Bittner, don't do that," he said with his comically imploring croak, for a vague fear advised him to experience Wiest's subsequent outbursts without a witness. "You have some practice in the treatment of seasick people, but Wiest is not one of the usual sort. I think that if another arrives, it will create a disaster."

The head barman had opened the door to the room a crack and was listening through it. Now he bent over with laughter and smacked his hand on his knee.

"A mad Christian!" he murmured admiringly. The bank manager interrupted himself and hurried to him. "What's happening now then?" he asked.

"Well just listen, now he is over by the pair," the head barman whispered and wedged his ear still firmer into the crack.

Suddenly the furious voice of the stranger was heard.

"You're a shameless, indecent lout," he shouted and pushed away a chair. "One more word and I'll box your ears like a young guinea pig."

Klöhn shook, shoved the head barman to the side and closed the door behind himself.

An excited conversation could be heard, then the dispute seemed to calm down, and after some minutes, Klöhn came out with the lovers. The girl first, pale and outraged, behind her the bank manager, openly cheerful about "the interesting food put out" that he experienced.

"What did he say then?" he asked the "bridegroom" and gave him his ear.

"Smut, but full," he whispered, "of sexual points and things. My bride didn't know where to turn. It may well be! But you have to respect people!"

He offered his lady his arm and disappeared with muffled indignation, escorted to the door by Bittner.

Klöhn watched after the strangers almost with envy.

"Who is the gentleman?" he asked the returning hotelier and made an elegiac nose after a sighed clearing of his throat.

"Ah, I believe, a dispatcher with Wöllmer," he answered somewhat sniffily.

"Thus a porcelain man," Klöhn said smiling ironically and disappeared with the words, "Well, now I'll make the last cool compresses for my patient. Hopefully it won't take long, and if it works somehow, direct the newly arriving guests to the meadow."

He pointed grinning at the room opposite which was furnished entirely in green.

Then he let the door close creaking behind himself. You could hear how he jogged the lock from within, testing it, and then how his circuitous steps tailed off into the room. The head barman wanted instantly to put his ear to the door, but Bittner waved him away.

"I don't want my guests to be eavesdropped on," he said going into the hall. "I'll take over the serving of both men myself this evening. Tell the number two as well."

Bittner wound the clock and saw that the time stood at three quarters to twelve.

Yawning, he ducked into his private room. The bar men were crouching in dark corners, the gas lamps were humming and a drowsy whirl sometimes came over their light.

— — — —

When the bank director Klöhn returned to the large, round table, the engineer was still leaning against the wall, rigid, stiff, with head sunk down, only his body had slid somewhat sideways and abided like a tipped over stake in the corner formed by a wall projection.

Klöhn acted as though everything was in order at the table, took a deep draught from his glass and then looked up as if by chance at the motionless drinker. With his searching eyes, he straightaway met the engineer's eyes, which, burnt out and cryptic, seemed to have waited the whole time to meet his.

Now they were touched by the bank manager's glance, the rigidity eased from his body and Wiest sank with a pitiful sigh in his seat, as if he were falling to the ground, but was caught by the stiffening of his arms on the table, held himself on the bench, sat upright and nodded contentedly that he had succeeded.

He has become deliriously drunk or crazy, the bank manager thought and sensed that he himself was not completely sober anymore.

"Listen, Wiest, it's probably quite enough for you!" he said therefore, and the tone of his voice was involuntarily brutally biting.

"Why?" the engineer asked dully without stirring.

"Well, I have just heard everything folding up with you ... really folding, you know. — I think we should stop and go home, that is, if you don't want to tell the story from the start. You hound! That would soon have become a nasty meal with the salesman if I hadn't have come in, hahaha!"

When the bank manager's laughter had died away, the engineer looked at him from the side. Then he said,

"That's right, it's just the two of us ... but just for that reason, there's still something to say."

With that he stood up decidedly and walked past the table with an elongated assuredness through the room, as if he had been seized by something invisible under the shoulders, and his feet seemed to walk on air.

"You certainly have cheerful legs, man," Klöhn called, watching him exactly, laughing out loud, "now stop the boozing."

Wiest did not pay any attention, but instead bolted the door.

Something like concern stirred the bank manager when he saw that, and he had attempted to hurry and hinder the engineer from it. Only Wiest had so lost his poise on the way back to the table that he staggered miserably and had a face like a wrung out, yellow rag which has been hung out to dry.

For that reason, Klöhn slunk back to the bench, laughed off his fright softly, clenched his right hand vigorously a few times under the table and thought, "Ha, I'll crumple him like a botched receipt form if it comes to that."

"So, now finally let it out," he said out loud when Wiest had taken his seat again.

The engineer shut his eyes as if he was going to sleep. His breath became restful and lulling. Suddenly he shook his head and smiled. Without looking up, he said softly, "It's especially difficult."

"What is?" the bank manager asked.

The engineer grasped his lower lip with thumb and forefinger and turned it over meditatively. Then he began, "With life it conducts itself like with a wheel set in motion. So long as it is moving, it can know nothing of itself, and when it stands still, it can't either because then it is dead."

Wiest spoke softly and, sitting unnaturally stretched, gazed straining continuously at the floor between him and Klöhn.

"Only the wheel preserves in the point of friction of its axle a consciousness of its rotation which is admittedly only possible through the diametrically opposed state of the other part, that is, the axle. See, Klöhn, and so there is also an axle in men, around which the madness of our live's spokes are continually flickering. It doesn't participate, the axle, haha, never, I tell you. Why? Dammit — ... I say, dammit ... No, it doesn't participate ... Listen!" He leaned forward and whispered mysteriously, "For it goes through the heart of God."

Klöhn drew his fat brow into obtuse bulges and said to himself, "Completely *tremens*."

"That is, of course, extremely uninteresting for you," Wiest said malevolently as if he had waited in vain for an answer. "But let that well be, it continues. You know, everything has the axle in itself, be it cardboard or cardinal, all the same. The music climbed from there to Beethoven, the religion to the saints, the new machines to the great inventors, and those who are not capable of anything else, from there they make the children of love."

Klöhn's face lit up cheerfully. — "You're a sod with your axle! Haha, godly! Beautiful, I give way to you! So that is your creation point," he sputtered meanwhile.

The engineer faltered astounded and then continued with hostile sharpness in his voice, but composed, "There are men whose view sinks to the depths of their inner being. They are then condemned to live like a dreamer who sees himself from a window perpetrating all sorts of stupidity, feels madly ashamed over the trifles, stupidity and despicableness which his golem wangles there in front of him and yet cannot hurry to stop him. You know, bank man, such men also see the golem of others, that living harlequin, and at the same time the shameful face of the ape's owner who watches the animal's sordid capers."

He interrupted himself and looked at Klöhn scornfully.

Then he continued, and it seemed as if he bit through each word with fury, "But it gets even better, dear ... haha ... dear Mr Klöhn. Do you understand, some men don't have this face in the window, not anymore ... not yet ... that I know, haha. They are just long-tailed monkeys and baboons and pricks and ..."

The engineer was choking on his fury, his lips had become completely bloodless, his yellow mongol face was contorted.

The bank manager sat there sententiously and composed.

"How?" Wiest hissed, barely in control of himself anymore, and shoved his fist on the table towards Klöhn. It was pale and emaciated like a ball of string.

"Keep to yourself," Klöhn said with the calm menace of a bulldog. "With me you are coming to a dead end. It'll soon be busted."

"What? You cart load of lard and sleepy swin-
ishness ... You want to laugh at me ... do you?!"

The engineer's entire body was shaking. But
Klöhn now really erupted into ungovernable
laughter so that the tears ran down his cheeks.

When he could look up again, a complete
metamorphosis had taken place in the engineer.

He was sitting recoiled, horrified and helplessly staring at the bank manager.

"Yes, yes, my friend! So behave yourself,"
Klöhn said triumphantly.

"... And at the same time, you know, you must
know that I know everything?" Wiest asked
mutely.

"Now you see, now you can speak forthwith
quietly," the bank manager interrupted him and
stroked his forehead. "For my sake, say by the
way whatever you want."

"You are crook ... The deposits you have are
embezzled ..." Wiest said quietly.

"Well. Very good, continue," Klöhn said
scornfully. "I still want to help you. I got you so
stupid ten years ago that you bought the Birkenfelder preference shares for fifty thousand. Not
so? But you want to get that out, you whinger."

The engineer was suddenly overcome by a
ghostly, eerie silence. His eyes faltered, extinguished deep in his head.

"Yes," he said unflinchingly quiet, "you had
bought the paper the day before for loose change

because you knew precisely that the works could only stay above water for fourteen days."

"Haha!" Klöhn laughed stalwartly and continued amused. "Of course. Precisely so. And stuck your good money in my pocket. Yes. Excellent!"

"No, only thirty thousand. For as you know, the shares were caught after the merger with the Thedener works against all expectations at 21."

Klöhn had turned pale.

"Tell me. But all joking aside now ..."

"No joke!" the engineer cut off his words icily. "Here I have it in black in white." With that he touched the breast pocket of his coat.

"Ah, you mean Chodziesner, the rogue?"

"A rogue too, certainly, but a more prudent one. Yes, precisely he who had given you the information about the Birkenfelder works at the time and lowered the plunder a quarter for it. He who beat it to America and is the lead hand today for "Nuther and Sons" in Buffalo. The letter which he wrote to you at the time cost me his passage. Your raiding assistant ..."

"And you think someone will believe you," Klöhn laughed spasmodically. "I advise you to go see a shrink. Mr Wiest! Yes, or why don't you denounce me if everything tallies so?"

The engineer's pupils began to twitch again. With trembling hands, he grasped the table edge and pulled himself up arduously from the bench and looked down in front of himself for a long time sorrowfully.

Then he raised his head, looked the bank manager in his now pale, haggard face and answered with faltering words, "... Yes, yes ... hm ... I ... must have laughed over it for ten years ... and did not comprehend it ... and boozing ... and did not comprehend it ... but you had utilised the municipal teachers' deposits for your profit and needed my money to cover it ... and if I did not keep quiet, you would be sitting eight days later behind lock and key ... yes ... and your daughters would be on the street ... the 'beautiful sisters' ... man ... I saw God's thorn bush burning at the time sometimes in the one, sometimes in the other ... that's right, and I was making fire, some-times in the one, sometimes in the other ... but steady ... dammit ... yes ... and let my parent's money fall in your rogue's sack ... man ... I'm God's ass ... I am ... I am ..."

The bank manager lay with both his elbows propped on the table and stared stupidly and crumbling at Wiest, whose face looked like that of a dying man going to battle death.

"... Klöhn! — Klöhn!!" The engineer screamed like someone screaming for help. He had sprung up and was holding his arms outstretched be-seeching and consecrating. Then he sat down like a knife snapping shut, moved quite close to the motionless bank manager and whispered in his ears, "... I am, I am ... son of my father ... help to a forger and rogue in order to rescue whores ... How? — I coerce God to clean Satan's closet ..."

"D...d?" Klöhn asked slurring, and clenched his teeth.

"... With my parent's savings, a procurer ..." the engineer murmured and drew his head down into his shoulders.

"D...d?" Klöhn asked trembling again. Tears were running over his cheeks. At the same time, a deathly determination arose in his fat face.

Slowly, noiselessly, he rose, more like a gorilla awakening from his sleep, and moved with eerie calm towards Wiest, who had also risen quickly and was backing away with the smile of a mad-man.

"D...d? ... D...d? ..." Klöhn asked quieter and quieter, and his lower lip hung down limply.

Now Wiest bumped into the corner of the walls. He sat firmly. — — — —

The barman had run into the yard on Wiest's scream and was watching the two from the roof of the shed. Suddenly he saw the engineer set off towards the bank manager like a snake and drive with his scrawny hands at his fat throat. With a tremendous crack, the men fell entwined in a ball under the table.

A wild fear seized the boy. With the cry, "Help! — Help!" he ran back.

When they entered the door of the room, the engineer was already standing in the middle of the room again, pale, with an unrecognisable face, looking at his raised hands and smiling madly.

Nobody dared approach him.

They went around him and found Klöhn lying lifeless under the table.

Before a stout-hearted man could take hold of the engineer, he threw his arms sideways and began singing with the whining voice of a maniac, "*Ite ... missa est* ... Father ... God ... *ite ... ite ...*"

Then he staggered out of the room like someone blinded. Outside the room, he ran into the wall of the hallway, collapsed and continued singing softly and sobbing.

The Grandmother

Old Mrs Kleideck, the surviving spouse of the teacher and cantor Johann Marianus Kleideck from Wenzelsdorf, had in her youth been a girl in love with life, high-spirited even. But fate allotted her the ill favour of fulfilling the first love of her undeveloped heart. She married at seventeen. And when she arose after weeks from her first childbirth, she was in the midst of the afflictions of a sorrowful life, which was at fault for her turning odd in her old age.

Since the death of her husband, who, betraying all hopes, voluntarily parted from life, she lived in Falkenstein, a middling town of the High Ash Mountains, and soon belonged because of her whimsicality to the eccentrics of this place.

She walked about, even on the hottest summer days, in a black shawl which she wore drawn over her head so that seldom did anyone see her face.

Nobody knew what she sought wandering about restlessly in the streets. And when a passerby talked to her, she paused in her progress, though as if she was doing it as a matter of a hidden, innate need, waited for the words of the other and then continued on her way without answering or unveiling her face. Only if someone told her of a terrible case of misfortune and took pains to visualise every horror properly did she then raise her head attentively, and her plump face lay still as if surprised by an unexpected light. In the progress of the narrated horrors, the initial radiance transformed into the greatest pleasure. Her eyes shimmered, her mouth stammered suppressed sounds of happiness, and she had to press her mouth shut with her fingers as if it were only possible through use of this external force that she could restrain a loud outbreak of jubilation. When this state occurred, the seventy year old tended not to show the least interest in her immediate surroundings anymore for days. She walked about withdrawn as if meditating, sought out dark corners and, while she waved up and down with her right hand as though caressing the shadows, she whispered tender words. Her preference for incurable illnesses, suffering faces distorted by pain, her yearning after the crying and lamenting of others were just as well-known and incomprehensible to the people as her fear of joyful people, the fright which all mirthful laughter gave her.

Otherwise she was quite normal, fetched her small widow's pension at the appointed hour, signing with her young, girlish handwriting, kept herself and her little room clean and never forgot to gift the obligatory taler on birthdays to her children strewn all over Germany. But any happy fate for all these people whom her body had borne obviously did not concern her at all. She had no mind for the advancement of her sons and the favourable changes in the lives of her daughters. She held the letter with the happy news, after she had read it, for a long time in her motionless hand in her lap and looked helplessly at nothing. Then she stood up and scurried to the oven. Only when the paper had gone up in flames and smoke did she breath out and could turn herself over to the old, dead certainty.

But whenever and wherever illness darkened the light of the rooms in her children's apartments and had the doors moving soundlessly, she soon appeared on the threshold and gave a heartening nod to the sorrowful ones. Her silent mouth became talkative, and whereas otherwise the words were joined together under great pressure as if they had been wrested arduously from forgetting, now the talk flowed rejuvenated from her lips which turned full of blood, and her short, plump body moved about with great ease. Her faith in herself grew with every turn for the worse. When the sick person lay pale and exhausted in the pillows, lips dry from heat, eyes rigid and wide in fever, then the old woman sat, the limp, moist hands of the poor one held in her own, and hummed softly and wistfully between her lips a cheerful song. She was tireless in her care, inexhaustible in the invention of new mitigations. But when the shadow of death moved in then she used her last resource. What that actually was, nobody knew to say, and the old woman herself steadily refused to give any information. She shut herself in the patient's room with the person fated to die and remained there for hours. The people listening fearfully at the door heard nothing except from time to time her words which sounded stretched out as though in song.

Her children thought she had come into mysterious powers through her difficult life and "critiqued" the illness. For that reason, the trust in her help was unbounded. For nobody languishing in dying, at whose bed she had sat, had yet been taken by death. All the children and grandchildren who had been lurching to the grave had imbibed their being from this old, enigmatic soul for a second time.

When the sleep of recovery came over the sick persons, then the grandmother began to ossify again. Her face became spiritless, her eyes lacklustre and empty, her words broke up in her mouth again before they found their way by untoward tongue over her lips. She hauled herself arduously about and when the saved person stood upright again in the midst of the happiness of their own, the old woman collected together her belongings and parted with a dreariness from them as if the people had been lost to her by the blessing which she had called forth herself. No word, no thank you reached the absent one. She heard everything said to her in a dull lethargy as if she understood nothing.

But from every victorious battle against the torment of life, she returned strengthened to her lonely little room, and the people thought that if fate does not forget to now and then send one of her relatives a deadly plague, the strange woman will not even die. And really, it had the appearance that these mockers could be right.

The years did not only pass by the old woman without trace, they even rejuvenated the unbreakable woman. The fullness of her body disappeared, her face became thinner and took on the colour of weathered rocks. And even if her eyes were sinking deeper into their sockets and language seemed to be lost to her thin lips: her gait became free and easy like only confident people stride. In this tempo, she moved into her ninetieth year.

But we men know only that tomorrow is a day too. What it brings remains hidden from us. The future takes ever new steps in eternal circles.

Two months after her birthday, which fell in January, that is in the last days of April, the old woman disappeared once again from the town. The market basket with her belongings on her arm, a solemn light in her eyes, the gesture of lively words around her lips, she travelled to Upper Silesia to her youngest daughter whose husband occupied the post of registrar with the tax administration at Oppeln.

He was named Peschke.

A bit past two o'clock in the afternoon, she arrived at his apartment and found the man in the dim, narrow entrance, ready for duty, his coat buttoned up militarily, as he lifted his stick from the stand.

With her entrance, he walked about, examined her in the darkness with sharp eyes and, instead of replied to her greeting, said,

"Of course, the old one too! Well, for all I care, it's all the same to me now! Good day."

With that he turned towards the way out, bitter, laughing scornfully to himself. But when he arrived at the stair landing, he turned back once more, took the grandmother by her arm, drew her into a room, planted himself threateningly before her and threw it cuttingly in the face of the old woman,

"I did not call you, you understand? Martha did that behind my back again — yes — she who aids the frisky child in everything, no extra help — *extra* — help!! That's right, so it is! There's nothing wrong with the boy, with the damned boy! He is repeating a year again, and now he puts on an act: screams in the night and then lies as if he couldn't peep. — I know the little fruit better! Being lazy, learning nothing, playing himself away in the fashion. — That is what you get when you torment yourself and labour away so that the boy should have it better than ourselves. That's it ... that ... that *alone*!" He took his hat off, dried the sweat from his bare forehead with his colourful handkerchief and brushed with shaking hand a strand of grey hair across it. Then he intricately folded the handkerchief up again and pondered what there was still to say. But he found nothing, looked down lost for a while and then shook his head energetically as if he rejected in advance every attempt at indulgence.

The old woman did not seem to hear him at all, but stood by her basket and removed the things as carefully as if they were raw, vulnerable beings. When Peschke prepared to go, she turned around, raised her eyes to him and said with effort, "But it is serious!" The registrar correlated that with the boy's illness and asked with marked concern, "So, how do you know that?"

Mrs Kleideck gave him no answer and continued cautiously pulling her things out and laying them on a chair as if nobody but her was in the room.

Peschke murmured something about "all that women's tattle and nonsense" and went.

The grandmother now looked around the room, which she recognised as the kitchen, and opened the window as if all the air had been used up by her son-in-law.

In turning around, she saw her daughter standing in the doorway.

Both women acted as though estranged for a while.

Then the old woman took a step into the room. At this moment, her daughter flung her arms around her mother's neck, and her body instantly started shaking with sobs which combined laments, cries for help and despair.

The old woman straightened up at first, lightly shoved the hysterical woman away and seized her hand with a strong, reassuring grasp.

But her mouth did not flow over from the stream of cheerful comfort as was its art normally. That took from her daughter all hope so that the poor woman had to sit down on a chair and constantly struggle against sinking down completely by weakly straightening up.

The grandmother understood the helpless horror which distorted her child's face and looked to the door through which Peschke had left in order to make clear to the beset woman who was at fault that her words had to remain lying broken up in her mouth.

And then while her daughter Martha told with the haste of the scared of the illness of the fourteen year old Emil, its beginning and progress so far, so that everything became an accusation against her husband, the old woman stood without stirring a single feature of her face into lively sympathy, seemingly immobile. In truth, however, the ancient woman suffered in the knowledge that her soul was not blossoming as usual before the shadow of a dark fate, but rather calmly went on in its depths like a sound-less, impervious water. "... We ... ng ...will ... ng ... go ... to him ..." she said arduously and shoved her cold fingers into her daughter's moist, hot hand.

Before the door to the sick boy's room, the old woman bent down, laid a kiss on Martha's fore-head and caressed her temples softly with her hands so that her daughter seemed to barely feel a touch from it, rather just the wafting of a cool breeze.

Then she entered the room.

Even though she was careful, the door handle snapped loudly and the ill boy immediately cried out exhausted,

"Daddy! — Dear, good daddy! I will learn, will learn! ... will ... learn ..."

Martha hurried in and bent down to her child.

"Emil, look, Emil," she said in extreme loving goodness, "it's not your father. It's your dear grandmother."

Then the boy turned his face from the wall, raised his wide, fevered eyes to the old woman, smiled reassuringly and then moved his lips whisperingly and hastily as if he was memorising a lesson.

Mrs Kleideck led her daughter out and bolted the door, for her soul felt how close already to this tender life the dark waters were washing which carry us all away to never be seen again.

She realised that she had to immediately make use of the great means which were given to her. She hung the windows with heavy sheets so that it became quite dark, sat down on the ill boy's bed and covered his face with her cold hands.

After she had sat for a long time, she had in her depths the feeling of a heavy stone being moved away. Then she knew delightedly that the inner muteness was being taken from her, and the stronger the whirl of the disturbed, young life assailed her, the certainer she felt the sunken force of her own being climbing up in her.

The wondrous transformation which she experienced by every sickbed also began here to her joyful surprise.

She who had smashed her strength in hardship, whose life's pleasure had been destroyed in hunger, whose song had sweltered in deprivations, whose hopes had been blown away by thousands of disappointments, whose light had been extinguished in the darkness of inevitable worries: she slowly received it all back in return.

The little, sick boy's sighs, his groans, the failing of his exhausted heart, the exhaustion of his sweet strength: they tore up the great power of life from the deepest ravines of this old, ancient person, and hours later the grandmother sat in the colorfulness, the sunshine, the jubilation of an existence which she would have been capable of leading but which had remained denied to her.

She had been holding the thin little fingers of her grandson in her hands, and her rebirth, kindled by Emil's failing chest, flowed back again into them. The boy's expiring life embedded itself in the certainty which, a decaying, birthing dream, flowed streaming out of the old soul.

Towards evening the billowing of the re-awakening became so strong in the ancient woman that the jubilation constricted her chest. So as not to suffocate and in firm belief in the saving power of her reborn being over it, her ear already listening for the call, she started the ceremony her relations called "the critique".

She bowed, driven by a mysterious force, over the ill boy and poured the fervour of her life's ardency over the boy's pale face.

With gentle, imploring voice, she said singing,

"Child! — Child! — I have water in me which does not trickle away and flowers on which the wilting passes away. In the night, my happiness is preserved. From my roof, misfortune sinks countless times and does not destroy me. The mountains in which my youth played still bloom. Child, lift your heart, lift your soul! The winds take life and bring it. I have in me the mouth of a sea and drink all the streams and waters of your silence, your fading, your death. My heart nourishes itself on your fear and takes it from you.

I want you, my child, to live — live — live!"

Thus she spoke in whispers, bowed over the ill boy. With outstretched arms she lay over the child, and her eyes were wide open, her mouth overflowing with that power which, according to the legends, belonged to the old women of our remote ancestors.

The poor boy lay pale and calm. His breath had become deep and steady, and as the old woman laid his hands back on the bedcovers, they remained still and no longer trembled with the fever's pulse.

The grandmother now sat on the chair next to the bed, her arms propped on her knees, her hands entwined, and averted her face in expectation, the way someone views a wide, sunny land from a high mountain. While her eyes went over the expanse of her youth, fond, tender, intoxicated words fell from her mouth, sometimes rising up into songs, sometimes concluding again in the silly play of sounds with which children talk in inexpressible dreams.

The air in the room was soon full of this incorruptible life, like the scent of fresh meadow flowers or the breath of fountains just born, and the boy slept as if he lay in the shadow of a tree whose leaves had just been opened by the morning breeze.

In the entrance, the door opened. With cautious steps, two men entered who conversed quietly, standing in front of the ill boy's room, but then continued on again to the kitchen. She heard the voice of her joyfully excited daughter ring out, but, soon submerging again in the blossoming images of her inner being, everything around her sounded in the tones of a happiness never lived.

Then there was a knock on the door. At first timid, then louder and louder, fiercer. At first Martha called her name with imploring voice. She heard it vaguely through the intoxication of her dream. Finally Peschke banged heavily on the latch.

Emil came with a sigh out of his sleep. Mrs Kleideck rose, staggered as though drunk and opened the door. The glaring light of a lamp fell into the room. The old woman staggered back blinded and luckily fell back on a chair in which she stayed, shading her eyes with her hands.

"Please, Professor Manczik, if you will kindly allow, I will lead the way with the lamp," she heard her son-in-law say.

"Yes, yes, just go," a blustering, old voice replied. "So he has been sick for two days."

"Yes, Professor," her daughter now answered apprehensively, but as gently as she could.

"He always has a terrible fear of mathematics. I think then ..."

Manczik interrupted her,

"Where then is your grandmother?"

Peschke whispered something to which the professor answered with an ironically stretched "Hm — hm".

Now they wanted to stand by the bed.

"Good afternoon, Peschke," the mathematics teacher said with a friendly voice. "Don't you recognise me? I'm your teacher — Professor Manczik. — He seems to be asleep."

"Oh, but his eyes are wide open. Nonsense!" the registrar spoke.

"I ask you, husband, don't shout so," Martha asked. "Don't you see it? — Leave him, otherwise we'll agitate him again."

"Well, he can speak though with his dear teacher. The professor had the goodness to come up with me. It won't be too much for the rascal if he shakes hands with the man. It hasn't been so bad with him in a long time. I've been sick too." — "Emil!" he called louder.

The boy emitted a long, fearful sound.

After a pause, the professor said,

"I think we should let him rest. Your wife is right." And, perceptibly relieved, he added, "If you keep him in bed a few days, I believe, he'll get better again. In spring all kinds of such things happen to children."

Peschke coughed roughly.

They moved to the door and Mrs Kleideck watched through the gaps between the fingers that she held in front of her.

"There is your grandmother. — Good evening, mother! Well, how is it then here in Oppeln?" she heard the professor say.

The old woman suddenly had such a fury at the unfamiliar man that she did not stir and kept her hand before her eyes.

Peschke laughed scornfully and said,

"Ah, come, Professor. The strongest man will get nothing out of her."

Manczik went, led out by the registrar, and the door shut again. Then it was silent. Silent and dark. In every darkness, a last breath of light swings trembling, ensuring that our eyes can perceive it. From the darkness which was left behind in the room, this last inkling of brightness had also disappeared.

Around the old woman, a solitary, inexpressible abyss had emerged. Her hands fell heavily into her lap and she was distressed in her soul so that her eyeballs hurt as they had many, many years before when she could still cry. She sat thus in dull trembling and thought of what would now have to happen with the ill boy and her, because the storm of healing song had been interrupted so roughly.

Meanwhile Peschke entered again with the lamp, carefully bolted the door and coughed with suppressed roughness like furious men who are resisting an emerging agitation are wont to do. Then he headed for the bed with decisive steps without paying any attention to the old woman.

She, however, stood up soundlessly and stepped behind him, driven by worry and the desire to help.

Emil still lay stiff in bed, his eyes fearfully directed at the covers, his hands balled into fists, his thumbs clenched in his fingers. The registrar placed the lamp on the chair. "Boy," he then said with strange tenderness, "boy! Where do you hurt actually? Well, just tell me! If you can open your eyes, you can open your mouth too. — Emil, I'm not doing anything to you. I just want to tell you something. Professor Manczik said you'll be better soon. I will let you have hours! — You! — — — Thunderbolts, I'm not your fool!!!" This furious eruption lifted the boy up. He knelt in bed, raised his hands to heaven and with a shaking calm voice, he began as if praying fervently,

"Ulisses in eroibus suis venit ad Aeoliam insulam in qua Aeolus, rex ventorum, habitabat. Insula firmo nurra cincta erat. Aeolus clemens erat adversus. Ulissem et eum de Troia et de Graecis interro — ga — ga — ..."

He broke off stuttering, tried coughing to speak the difficult word, fell silent in trembling fright and finally fell back on the bed, his folded hands shaking in despair. With that he cried out piteously,

"Dear, good father, leave me. I want to die. I want to die!"

Peschke stretched out his hand straightaway to pull the ill boy up by the shoulders and teach him "how it is".

Then he felt his wrist clenched by an ice-cold wizened hand and pulled back. When he turned around, he looked into the shrunken face of the ancient woman. It was pale. The hate in the deep-set eyes made it terrible. She looked at him thus for a while, then she said with imperious contempt, "Go immediately!" and turned his hand to the door.

The boy was stammering his cry for death constantly, quieter and quieter.

Peschke moved to the door with the lamp. There he composed himself from the fright which the weird old woman had dealt him, and he called with the empty defiance of the chastised to the bed of his son,

"For my sake, die. Better to have a dead child than a disobedient one."

After his disappearance, it was silent again in the room and Mrs Kleideck stood upright, holding fast in her embrace the back of the chair.

The boy whimpered, pining, and the old woman felt his despair as hot, consuming waves beating in her face.

At this moment, her daughter entered the room. The aged woman stood stiffly and did not stir. Her eyes lay so deep in their sockets that they seemed to have been driven into her head by a slingshot. Finally the spasm which had seized her eased.

She laid her hand on her daughter's shoulder and said comforting,

"Go sleep, I'll calm him down again," straightened herself up and repeated, protracted and stronger, groping towards a decisiveness, "*I'll calm him down*. That's right! — But your husband mustn't come in again." Then she blew a kiss on her daughter's forehead so that Martha went out consoled.

The large apartment building became silent. On the streets, the steps of late home comers echoed. By the sheets, pale stripes of light flowed into the room, for the moon was climbing over the rooves.

From the room next door, she heard now and then the rough voice of Peschke which forced her every time to look at the floor.

Once when she looked up again, she felt a skimming in the air and was also able to perceive it after some time as a grey raiment which flew through the room like a rider's fluttering cloak.

The wall to which it moved in great speed gave way into endlessness. A subterranean, dark passage yawned open in whose depths a cadaverous light began to smoulder and rolls of thunder came from the vaults of the passage like the drumming of ghostly, racing horses' hooves. The haste of the apparition grew as if it was carried by an intensifying storm. And now, at the last moment, the old woman could perceive clearly the figure of a grey rider who, bent forward racing, sat on a chestnut stallion. Before he was lost in the vertiginous expanse, he turned his head to her and smiled lovingly at her with his hollow, fleshless face.

Then the grandmother knew that she had seen death and what fate wanted for the boy and her.

She closed her eyes and sank onto the chair. For a long time, her breath skipped as though in great fright.

But strangely, as her heart again began roughly to beat regularly, she was not torn to a new struggle with death over the ill boy.

No, it seemed to her again as if she was sitting on a high mountain and her eyes, looking down, saw a land quite far off beneath her. Houses stood there between blossoming gardens, paths meandered through the greenery and people were going back and forth on them. Finally she recognised that it was Wenzelsdorf and in its features, she surveyed once more its entire life.

In the end, she caught sight of herself strolling out of the village and climbing up the mountain on which she sat.

And, strangely, all the difficulties and distress which she had experienced and suffered had lost their dread and horror. Her life lay in happiness and beauty before her; immersed in a high, gentle light, all distortions from hardship smoothed out so that she asked herself astounded again and again,

"Yes. Was my life like that? Was it like that?"

And she did not understand how it had been possible that her eyes had been able to veil by the bloom of the pain the radiance, the splendour which in truth every human body is.

Although she knew quite exactly that these unusual thoughts within her and these images around her were nothing but the process which people call dying, she was no more excited than a golden-ripe leaf on a tree which feels itself in the quiet autumn sun being separated from the branch.

All that remained to her of the terrestrial was a last astonishment which she would experience when the being was with her which she had seen climbing the mountain and who was none other than herself.

The nearer she came to herself, the greater her faith in the eternal and infinite which she saw opposite her, and with a jubilation which she barely overmastered, she recognised that the existence through which she had stridden lay like a golden ring around all the world's vitality. This knowledge of her deepest soul intoxicated her so that a rejoicing took place around her like the thunder of a festive tolling; as if heaven had opened its breast and was calling her up to itself with a great storm of jubilation.

The aged woman had been quite shaken by it and thought of what must become of the boy if he must stay behind on the earth. But her grandson, Emil Peschke, lay silent; in his face, a cheerful happiness was clustering and through his body, the last stirrings of life were running.

At the same time, the room filled wrenchingly quick with radiant light.

As the grandmother raised her face to see what was happening, she noticed the dark sheet glide from one of the windows to the ground, and in the opening, appearing large to her like a mighty gate, the image of a transfigured spirit appeared and immediately began to float towards her. It had opened its arms and was slowly approaching her.

"Is that me? Is that the eternal in me?" the grandmother asked timidly.

The godly being nodded.

"And the radiance, is that the eternal day?"

Her transfiguration did not answer her anymore with a gesture. It approached Mrs Kleideck slowly but surely. When it had come so near that the old woman sensed the radiance like a searing fervency over her entire body, she tore the boy to herself, embraced him and let herself sink into the abyss of light.

***

Mrs Peschke had not been able to sleep all night from heartache over her only boy and constantly asked in worry what would happen if her mother was no longer up to the illness.

Towards morning a thin skin of dreaming crept over the eyes of the registrar's poor wife.

Into this dawn, the town's morning bells rang. When they stopped, she awoke completely and went up to the ill boy's room to see how her son was.

There the grandmother and Emil lay entwined in each other's arms, both dead.

The aged woman's countenance still gleamed and the eyes of her dead boy sparkled mischievously from under his fallen eyelids.

For that reason, the woman did not break into tears. She sank down to her knees by the bed and put her face in her hands.

The Spirit of
the Father

In the industrial town of Waldenburg from which he originated, Doctor Florian Brustat had given a public lecture over his research trip through the region of those Arctic tribes of Siberia which are quickly dying out under the advance of Russian civilisation as if seized by a deadly illness. He had not appeared for the sake of profit in his hometown, but to offer his patron, the businessman Ihme, the satisfaction of having his steadfast patronage towards him shown subsequently to be justified before the audience of the leading circles of the town, and to not spare the shame of the philistine bourgeoisie. The negotiations over the bringing about of the lecture had been carried out between protege and patron with delicacy and irony so that neither the one from boasting, nor the other from the feeling of belated bitterness, felt himself encumbered. Old Ihme, already a little uncertain from age, had probably been the first to shake the speaker's hand thankfully at the conclusion of the lecture, but had then been shoved aside by the swarm of loud admirers and flushed down the stairs so that he seemed forcibly to walk on air, had climbed smiling into his carriage and slowly rolled to his house which lay in a park-like garden outside the town.

It was a tepid autumn night, dark, and yet lit by a glassy clarity aloft which could be seen now and then through rifts in the clouds of smoke. The chimneys did not stop swirling their dark ensigns over the rooves. The white haze from the coking plants rolled in from the north. A gently clamouring seething was in the air. Now and then, the signal from a pit cried out whinnying like a tortured, brazen horse, and then the dull roar of the hauling engines were heard more clearly again from the earth's interior, cautiously growling so that you seemed to feel it as a gentle vibration in the legs.

Doctor Brustat had let himself be abducted by his friend, the mayor Musiol, into the small garden which, behind the town hall with its dozen trees, its summerhouse, its handful of paths and benches, was bordered on the one side by windowless house walls, abutted on the other side by a connecting road and left free at the back the view over the roof of the high school to the nearby Laxenberg.

Both men had been joined by Musiol's friends, the judge, Wiese, and the school principal, Leutner.

The table had been carried from the summer-house and placed on the lawn under a broad, old apple tree.

At Brustat's request, the hurricane lamps had been extinguished, because in his opinion the men's faces took on a spasmodic expression in that lighting. "You know, gentlemen, us Europeans", the explorer said, "do not have the physiognomies which can bear up in the unease of such light. Cultured men are missing the inner collectedness. They respond without knowing to the flickering and flux."

"But we can drink nevertheless, Florian," the mayor said laughing, "can't we, Wiese? When we are Europeans too. Cheers! Old, dear traveller of deserts and shamans. It's magnificent that we have you here again!"

They clinked glasses together, and then a silence arose from the hidden striving of the judge and school principal to recognise something of Brustat's facial expression through the darkness.

"Yes, actually why didn't you return with the Siberian railway?" Leutner asked after a while.

"Certainly, it would have been easier," Brustat answered with his deep, steady bass, from which the powerful bulk of his figure and the large, sober face of the famous researcher could be fairly heard. "But, what does easier mean, gentlemen?! I simply had to return across through Asia. It had no chance against that. It made sense to trace the old trade routes which had connected China with the West, that is Europe, as far back as is known."

"Not possible! Really!" the judge threw in between. "And then the likes of us think that the English sprung the yellow gate open first in the fifties of the past century."

"Yes, yes!" Brustat laughed good-naturedly over Wiese's sharp, abrasive voice. "But you see that some have read Strabo and Ptolemy and rarely does one know it exactly. No, it is not to be doubted that between the Tian Shan and Kunlun mountains on the southern road or Nanlu, the Chinese in all the centuries carried out a lively trade with the West, with Europe. It is incidentally also, I presume, the road which Strabo and Ptolemy described.

Moreover, speaking of later times, the legation of Ganthun from Tatsin is none other than that of the Roman emperor Antony. In addition, you will also have certainly heard about the legation of Dissabulus to Justinian."

"Not a trace!" Leutner replied laughing out loud. "You create a false idea of what is in the head of today's average middle European."

"Tell me, Florian, is it true what I read recently in the 'Silesian' that you really have command of fifty languages?" Musiol asked.

"Oh, you know, when you have the first ten," Brustat replied, "then it works by itself. Yes, it could be a few more if you count dialects."

Above the crowns of the trees, the red reflection of a coking plant now twitched. The restive wall of haze shook aloft and trembled as if in the frisson of fever.

Brustat rose and stepped to the edge of the garden, as if to be nearer the reddish wall of haze above. He was probably also eschewing the amazed questioning, for since he had become in the judgment of his contemporaries the "phenomenal arsenal of all knowledge", the looks of all men smacked against his face like slaps in homage.

The remaining men conversed quietly, and Wiese pressed Leutner almost violently into his chair to stop him following the researcher who was lost in meditation. "For," he said, "you did not observe the expression in his eyes during the entire lecture, which locked themselves out from everything happening around them with their look, yes, even remaining aloof from everything that the speaker thought, said and did. Perhaps it is right when I say he looked at us from the eyes of an innocent man condemned."

Musiol and Leutner laughed gently over the incorrigible trial judge.

But Wiese stuck to his opinion. — "Why would he have had the hurricane lamps extinguished then? Yes!"

From the layer of haze above, which now shimmered turbidly, sulphurously pale and sickly with a breath of smoky red, a bright cloud swelled inexorably alone, independent, as if a white figure was stepping out of a burning house.

Brustat turned around with a gesture of passionate surprise and invited the three with a motion of his hand to observe the phenomenon. But they had put their heads together and were whispering.

That's why the watcher turned back to the sight above and observed that the white sky-fugitive, which had meanwhile faded, charred to a grey-black little heap, was lying before the long front of the fiery red house of clouds. With head sunk in thought, he returned to the table.

"Yes, where had we stopped?" the school principal began. "Right the trade route. Quite right. Well, and is it right then now with the prevailing of the French influence in Syria. You did come through Syria ..."

Musiol interrupted him though, "Oh where, Leutner, you ..." And Wiese entered for the mayor, "By all means, Alphons. You have had one of your daydreams. Mr Brustat was speaking of his journey by junk from Al Hudaydah to Jeddah. Ergo, Syria is impossible."

The school principal sprang up grotesquely and emitted a scornful laugh. But then he instructed the pair that a journey in the Red Sea did "not necessarily, irrevocably" exclude the choice of a land route through Syria.

Doctor Florian Brustat sat calmly in his place, held his head bowed still thinking and looked from time to time almost furtively at the layer of haze, which was now paling as if black veils floated over the roof of the high school and the Laxenberg, and now and then was streaked shimmering by the flash of the electric rail as if by a blue-green bird. He was entirely suffused by a hidden devotion.

"Now, we must in fact however appeal first to my most revered Florian Brustat as adjudicator before we bang our heads together," Musiol called wittily.

The researcher did not change his pose. He grasped his glass, drank and remained silent.

Wiese pushed the school inspector and gave him a nod as if to say, 'Well, wasn't I right about his eyes?'

"You are both right. I travelled back by the coast of Yemen, but then went from Jeddah by land through Syria," Brustat said finally and so conclusively that nobody felt any intent to let themselves go in ungoverned curiosity.

The judge had sensed correctly. Around the researcher there was a strange atmosphere through which he was carried far away as if made intangible.

And because the turnings in the men's conversation were always provoked by such hidden affairs of the soul, Musiol came to speak of the fact that Brustat was not actually born in Waldenburg, but came from Tannhausen, a village a few kilometers away.

"Legend," Leutner said, "or that old father Trübner, who showed me the birthplace of our famous Brustat on Charlottenbrunner Street, are suddenly becoming idiotic."

Brustat spoke, "No legend, Principal. The house of good Trübner is surely my father's house, but not my birthplace, even if my brother still lives there at present."

"Yes, but as ...," Leutner burst out, as a fanatic for contradictions like all schoolmen, to bear down on a scrutiny of the reasons for why Brustat's father had been induced to relocate, but he felt a resistance by which Musiol and Wiese impressed on him that he was on the point of entering on a delicate area.

To everyone's astonishment, Brustat resolved the tension of the uneasy moment by his deep, good-natured laughter. Then he said to Leutner,

"Dear Principal, don't let yourself in the least be embarrassed by the anxiety of the gentlemen. I know that both the revered men are guided by the best intentions. But I have an equally strong affection for men who bore through the hole untroubled to where they want. Oh, Musiol, why should I restrain myself in a point over which everyone else speaks so calmly? No, no! You see, my father went under in Tannhausen with his large milling business and rescued the rubble of his capital as a baker in the narrow house on Charlottenbrunner Street. That is all. A misfortune is no stigma, and if you take a good look at it, it was responsible for my becoming what I am. If you just want to afford yourself the pleasure of reflecting on the causes — — — which in essence certainly amounts to an illusion. For causes are *ad hoc* explanations."

If you could have seen the faces of the three men, you would have perceived in every one the expression of embarrassment.

Judge Wiese pulled himself together first and turned to the researcher,

"You will feel that we are flabbergasted by your sure awareness of, how shall I say it, the subterranean situation, Mr Brustat."

The researcher did not answer straightaway. Then he cleared his throat to begin. But Wiese ignored it, and beset by his own thoughts, he continued speaking.

"God, why should I stay behind the mountain! If I don't confess then I run the danger that you will pull the secrets out of my pocket, and I don't want to be the sheepish one. Just now when you were standing by the fence, I spoke to my friends of my observation during the lecture. I found in your eyes especially an expression of strangeness, as if, while you stood at the lectern acting with your arms and talking to us, you were not actually there in the hall and not Doctor Florian Brustat."

You could hear the gentle jerk with which Brustat turned to the speaker. But he still did not answer.

Leutner thus found an opportunity to pass in between, and said, "Why did you not tell the whole truth, Judge? He thinks you looked like an innocent man condemned."

Then everyone broke out into raucous laughter.

When silence had returned again, Doctor Brustat took up the conversation.

"Who wants to know? Perhaps Mr Wiese also is not in essence so entirely wrong about it, especially in so far as every man who has a fate to come before the broad public is such a thing as an innocent man condemned. For whoever really wants something, does not seek fame."

"But Florian!" the mayor said reprovingly.

"Yes, it isn't to be helped," Brustat said coolly. "You know, gentlemen, when you've resided for a long time among the people of the East, I mean in the real atmosphere of Buddhism, a fundamental change is implemented slowly and irresistibly in our inner being, and one beautiful day you find yourself alone in your being and absolutely bound to the universe, yet differently than through the fact of life. The 'Ingwa' or 'inner being', which means what to us Westerners comes in partial sense by the word 'Karma', forces itself on one at every turn. This idea is ever present there like the air. Constantly by day and night, this mysterious echo beats on our ear. I must explain myself more clearly to you.

Let us stay with the picture. The tone of western life is short, loud, violent. Like your gunshot, fired off in a narrow, enclosed space. If you live in the Orient for months, you notice that the existence of every individual is an affair of the universe, a sound which climbs out of the depths before us and loses itself in the matters after us without stopping.

You see, then you are, for example, Brustat and in addition another who sees from regions into this life of his, which then means nothing else for this second one than an instrument in a large orchestra, an instrument which is yourself.

I sense that you, Principal, are shaking your head in disbelief."

"Now yes," Leutner answered, "I understand you. You mean just now the suggestive power. Not this effect as fact, which would be considered our world view."

Brustat answered earnestly by falling silent.

After Leutner had been thus confounded, Brustat continued in his deliberations as if they had not been interrupted.

"At the same time, you end up in a state which really bestows on your eyes the expression of a strange, alien vastness. You have, Judge, really observed that correctly. For since my stay of many years in the East, my emotion goes deeper and deeper than my intelligence.

And believe me, I have won a delicacy which I heretofore only knew as idle dreams which my patron, the businessman Ihme, I assume, wanted to rid me of for the sake of my father and schooling.

But I think, gentlemen, that is enough now. I am starting to lecture. So, we break up!"

Brustat rose. But the three observed well the hesitance with which he stepped next to the chair, and assailed him not to savagely break off the marvellous conversation. The researcher fended off this praise from his listeners with a shake of the head.

"Marvellous, yes, for me more than you think," he said, taking his place again, "for you gift me the thoughts no less than I give them to you."

The others now shifted their chairs closer to the table again with the exception of Leutner, who was not able to evade the feeling of a small affront, but by the shadow of his aloofness, charged the tension which would progress the conversation with a mild hesitation.

Suddenly Brustat stretched his hand across the table and said gently,

"But before we wander further, Principal, offer me your hand. It did not lie in my intent to injure you when to your interjection I ..."

Leutner did not let him finish speaking. In his precipitant eagerness, he seized with both hands Brustat's right hand, shook and pressed it possessedly and stammered,

"You are too kind. Absolutely not. I thank you. I give my apologies many-times, Mr Brustat."

"So all is well," the researcher said simply. "I know your conviction, Mr Leutner, it is about the influence which the Eastern world view practises on the Westerner, about nothing else but the trespassing of a sheer illusion on uncertain souls, thus about a physically mechanical infection or suggestion, it is widespread, but I have experienced myself that it is really about more than some scent which you pick up on your clothes from another house and carry around for a shorter or longer time.

The belief in the pre- and post-existence, the conviction of a higher human essence which is not exhausted by the forms of its present being, has been demonstrated to me by an experience so insistent that since then I can no longer get to grips with it as quickly as with a mere suggestion.

According to my temperament and my profession so to speak as a philologist, I am in fact less amenable to romantic fallacies than thousands of others. Only, it's no use.

Just now, when I walked away from you and stepped to the fence, I was reminded of it again in a wondrously urgent manner by the view of a lit-up cloud. I saw in particular the clouds of smoke, which stand in quiet unease like a grey barrier over the Laxenberg, lit up red by the fiery glow of a block of coke cast out somewhere, as if it were the facade of a long, burning house. The glow soon blazed weaker and weaker. And when only a sulphurously burning light was dully thrown on everything, a white cloud stepped trembling out of the softly wavering wall and straightened up struggling like a being which seeks with its last strength for salvation.

You noticed nothing.

Of course, for habits are blackened glasses. But if you had also perceived it, each of you would have interpreted it differently.

However it reminds me of the death of my father.

Now, since you wished that our conversation was not yet finished, I was forced by you to perhaps disappoint, in that I am telling of what it drove me to and not what you probably expected. Only I concede to you the right to give my experience an interpretation which in the worst case could even be the opposite of flattering me."

Musiol interrupted the talker by an indignant exclamation,

"Be ashamed of yourself, incurable sceptic!"

And both the other men varied in their own ways loudly the protestation of absolute admiration and reverence.

But Brustat said smiling,

"That may be. Only you know how you are now, not how you will be at the end of my tale. I give you warning!

Though. Listen then:

It was at the end of my last journey through Cambodia and Indo-China. I returned by the ruined cities of Mesopotamia and intended to rest in Beirut through a stay of many days before entering the Western World, and to sample at leisure the spontaneity and naturalness of oriental human relations once more before I had to creep into the narrow fitted clothes of European social mores. Beirut is the seat of the nymph Beroe, over whom Dionysus and Poseidon once quarrelled in a pine wood which still stands close to the city, the old sanctuary of Baal-Berith, a place which with Alexandria, as a boundary between East and West, has much nastiness and is animated by a mix of peoples who seek the same. Which races they belong to, no Beiruter knows. Each vein smuggles itself from another region under his skin, each limb of his body has a different pedigree. That was the reason why I chose Beirut, the Girgash of King Baldwin, as the endpoint for my journey, I wanted to part with the fullest possible chord in my ear. Our caravan wound its way out of the sands of the Syrian desert towards midday, and the sun stood in the burning sky like a devil's skull scorched pale by a hellfire, when, after the longed for refreshing with water, we climbed down arduously into this valley of shade.

The last time, I had alighted in a greek-italian fonda, a sort of hotel, and I must say, the widow who managed it had understood her business. But, we were still not completely out of the room which we had inhabited, when a greek pontiff appeared and purified with holy water and biblical proverbs the rooms which had been contaminated by us heretical travellers. For that reason, I quartered myself this time in a native khan some distance out of the city. When the servant, down a long corridor, unlocked the room destined for me with the mace key, it didn't look confidence inspiring either. For the floor of the room was covered an inch thick by a filthy bark which, I don't know exactly, consisted of myriads of half-starved, vindictive little crea-tures. But the oriental also extends his tolerance to the smallest creatures, and so I took the mace key from the servant's hand and placed a few coins in his aged hand as an advance on the rent. Then my servant bore down on the room with a deluge and mop. It was laid with cheap mats, and so it was by mid-afternoon not very nice but made so that it could be moved into without any fear. My bed was laid as a divan next to the window, a clay water jar placed in the middle, I wrapped myself in the comfortable kief, stretch-ed out and supped the vapours of the sweet Latakia, the best Syrian tobacco from old Laodicea. After a while, my room neighbours, two Kurdish chiefs, came to visit me and took their places next to me on my invitation. They told very entertaining, whimsical bandit stories from the border conflicts with Turkey which Persia had engaged in at the time at the incite-ment of Russia and begun that occupation which the unfortunate kingdom has today half suc-cumbed to. In this way, the rest of the hot day passed pleasantly. Then I sat until nightfall near the khan in the shadow of a thick ivy shrub next to a small mountain stream, delighted in the view of the angular upper city, heard the muffled clamour ringing out from the quays, observed the ruins of old Berytus almost buried under climbing plants and, with the evening peals from the nearby monastery of the Maronites, passed into a dreaming which wasn't dissimilar to that which you succumb to after riding on a camel for many hours at night in the desert. It's as if the inner being flows apart in all directions to infinity, and only the gentle tone of the bells of the lead animal still gently maintains the sense of your person. I sat like that on the ground next to the khan, like on a rhythmically undulating camel's back which bore itself in rhythm with the monastery bells into an immeasurable infinity. And I, observing this, was soon myself bleared by sleep, it was thus no different than if two dream enthralled eyes saw themselves in the stars. I enjoyed comfortably for a while the immersion in this transitory sea and stretched my soul to all sides, finally feeling completely unwed by the merciless bridle of the will. Then I rose, but only with the intention of dissolving this state of waking dream into real sleep. In the khan's courtyard, I met my servant, who, walking before me with his little lantern, would lead me between balls of goods and over pieces of baggage into my apartments. Only it was easier meant than done, and when we stood happily before the long corridor at whose far end my room lay, we had to recognise the impossibility of progressing any further. Everyone, but also all the khan's guests had absconded from their rooms and had brought themselves back here with their pipes and watermelons. My servant probably made the attempt to wind his way through. But we would have literally had to climb over backs and heads if we had wanted to carry out the intention. For that reason, I called my servant back, laughing, and decided, because I now fancied myself pulled out of the unhurried dream whirl, to spend the time until my fellow guests went to bed in a walk through the streets of the upper city, so as to then calm myself in order to rest easier. My servant went down the stony path to the city with the point of light in front of me. From the oleander bushes and the mulberry bushes of Nahr al-Kalb in the valley below, swathes of coolness were already drawing, in the light of the half moon, here and there the river glittered, and the heights towards the mountains looked as if an inaudible stream of coolness was flowing from Lebanon down to us. But over the sea, the hot air still stood like an impenetrable wall.

Long rows of camels drew silently down to the harbour through the streets still protected and cooled here and there by carpets. Arabs strode soundlessly next to them or rocked on the laden animals' backs. In the arbours of the bazaar, Turks still sat silently in the glow of oil lamps behind their wares. From the full coffeehouses, shrouded figures glided noiselessly in wide burnouses. And if you hadn't heard from the harbour the singing of drunken sailors from the French cabaret, you would have tried to believe that the time of the steamships had lapsed without trace in these narrow dark streets and the city still lived today in the brilliance which the great Druze Fahreddin had brought over the land for the last time. The Orient is timeless. Yes, when we entered a small square-like extension around a street corner, I saw a scene truly like those from out of the thousand and one nights. There in fact sitting in the light of an oil lamp in a corner protected from the wind was an old man, from whose striking, reddishly lit face, the stream of a snow white beard flowed, and he was telling with a muffled voice some story to a small circle of men of various ages. The people were leaning motionless on the wall like stone figures darkened with age and listening silently. Only now and then did one or another stir into a gesture of emotion and then sink down again into the silence of listening which looked like the sleep of the spellbound.

Suddenly from the circle of listeners, a man stepped who I had not spotted up to then. He wore European clothes and, although already somewhat bowed with age, was almost herculean in build. The way in which he took the two, three steps over to us was so distinguishing and at the same time so familiar to me, that I looked at him sharply. But at this moment, he was gripped by a seizure. It constricted his body and he grasped for help with both hands in the air in the way that people suffocating do. But the danger to his breathing lasted only a few moments and cleared itself in a cough. With that the stranger stared exhausted across at me, stroked his mouth with the back of his large hand and set himself in motion staggering a little towards the next street, into the darkness of which he disappeared. Behind him a soft, indescribably enigmatic tone faded away.

I summoned my servant to follow the Frank who had just now been beset by ailment for a stretch and to fetch him back if possible.

But my servant just looked at me smiling and said that he had not spotted the shadow of a Frank here. Only Albanians and Beiruters were there. But the ghost horses of Ali had just trotted through my soul, he opined, by which he meant that I had succumbed to a trick of the senses.

I remembered my state in the dusk and agreed with him that the best means against such enchantments was 'a large, brimming cup of sleep'. Hence we made our way back to the khan.

Such a tiredness really overcame me after a few steps that I almost fell asleep on my feet. As I staggered half-dreaming, lead gently by my servant, it suddenly went through my mind like a bolt of lightning, 'That was your father, the Frank, that you saw.'

But I laughed in silence after the first quiet fright and thought it nothing but a persistence of that state of exhaustion and swayed serenely onwards on the arm of my faithful guide.

On awakening the next morning, the experience of the previous evening lay in pale, but distinct colours in my soul, like jellyfish swimming in the sea, of which I definitely knew that the marvel of their glowing rosettes would change into an invisible lump of slime if I scooped them up with my hand and brought them closer to my eyes. What I could have thought about this mirage on the horizon of my inner being for a long time! But I was for all that Brustat and not a bedouin. For that reason, there was no obligation for me to hear behind the experience the crunching of the universe's clock.

Nevertheless I took myself to the post office after my morning coffee and wired my brother here that I would receive an important telegram within the next eight days in Genoa. Then I went directly down to the harbour as if it had been my plan from the beginning, and reserved a place on an Italian steamer which started its journey to Genoa the next evening.

So perfectly was, unknowingly to me, the heavy weight of my soul displaced, that I saw nothing in the alteration of my departure but the implicit conditions under which I had composed it. It did not occur to me in the least to see in me a fellow who was lead by another force than my considered, cool will. Of a different opinion was the faithful brown fellow from Barbara, my servant on the journey there through Mesopotamia. His dedication, which in the last days had developed anyhow out of the servility of the inferior into free adoration, assumed straightaway the form of reverent awe, and on parting, already on the ship, he said, 'Sir, Allah has your hand in his own. He leads you on a good path.'

His face was not encumbered by any trait in its oriental stillness, only his black eyes shook with emotion when he pressed my hand to his chest for the last time, but then he clambered down the ladder to the boat quicker than was his custom, as if he was fleeing a danger. As soon as he felt the boards of the little boat under himself, he went into paroxysms of joy and he waved with both arms when the boat had already landed and our 'Marchese Deferrari' was drawing up its anchor rattling.

He had soon shrunk to a tiny grey-black little point. Our steamer, the good 'Marchese', struck out steadily. Beirut faded like a colourful cloth away from it. Not long after reaching the open sea, the red sun was pulled with a jerk under the horizon, and the colours of evening were chasing like a short, hectic fever across the water. Everything, sea, sky and ship, was instantly stuffed properly in a snatch into a black sack. We had a nasty night of storms. But despite the bluster, I did not stir from my cabin. I have broken the habit of fear on my many sea journeys, and the curiosity doesn't reward itself most of the time when it concerns European travellers who are in fear. The clapping of the sea whipping across the deck, the thundering of the sea on the bulkheads, the dull pounding of machinery, the howling of the wind, the shouts of the sailors calling things out in their work, the running around and moaning of the passengers; that all sounded like the many-toned rumbling of a rotating giant ball in whose middle I, as well as was possible, lay dressed on my bed. This drumming noise which revolved around me was penetrated by my glance if I closed my eyes, and I noticed that it was encircled by a belt. This latter made all the din sound to me like it was in the distance. A pale, quelled light also appeared, which stretched in pulses which flushed apart circles on the pond, further and further out and whilst this happened, a gentle tone rang, so gentle that all the noise around me fell silent before it.

And suddenly I remembered that it was exactly this tone which I had heard when the Frank had disappeared into the darkness of Beirut's lanes. The pale belt of light rang now exactly the same and tightened around the rotating ball of noise and flowed out further and further into infinity and abducted me in my soul with it, so that the turmoil of the storm sounded less and less distinct, in the end only dreamlike, as if from a high mountain.

In the late morning, the captain thundered on my door, "Doctor, are you dead or is something wrong with you?" Truly, I had slept through the entire, terrible night.

In Genoa I received my brother's telegram which read, 'Father very weak. Come immediately.' Four hours later, I sat in the express train from Ventimiglia; thirty six hours afterwards, I was in Berlin, climbing into the Silesian train, and I arrived about two o'clock in the afternoon before our narrow house on Charlottenbrunner Street.

My father had already died and lay washed, with chin bound up, on the bed of his small bedroom. The face peaceful, large in the closed transcendent expression of death, lit as ever by a mysterious light from the other side. Yes, even a weak victorious joy embellished the deceased's countenance. I stood by his bed and communed with him for the last time. Nothing of the hidden darkness filled this husk anymore, the darkness in which my father had secretly suffered since his business collapse and which in the last year had sometimes dimmed the clarity of his spirit so that he believed himself wronged by my brother and put his money in all kinds of ridiculous hiding places. He lay there serenely now, like after a walk in the open air.

And I, on whom it had been imposed by fate, despite all my successes, to be his deepest disappointment, because I had not joined in his business and had ceded the care for the family's reputation to my brother, to whom he trusted nothing in his blindness, I had the happiness to participate from a distance in his going in a mysterious way. Perhaps in this twilight hour of his existence, his eyes had been opened about me and the joy in my path and my way had lit his last moments.

While I devoted myself in the deceased's room to this short review, my brother, who had entered with me, went through the house and shut all the doors. When I left the body, he came down the stairs from the upper floor to me. We stepped into the living room, which had still been kept in all respects like my childhood had known it, sat down at the table, and my brother told me of the circumstances under which death had slowly gained dominion over my father. An old heart condition had plagued him more and more in the last weeks. But these fits, which had occurred more and more painfully, had been obstinately hidden from my brother by the old man, and even his housekeeper, with whom he resided altogether reclusively, was forced by him to only give out half indications. But six days ago, he had been beset by such a heavy attack that it had looked as if it was his last moment. Before going to sleep, towards nine o'clock in the evening, an asthma attack had overwhelmed him on the way to bed, and only after a terrible while did he escape the suffocation with a blue face and reddened eyes. I hid my agitation. For at exactly the same time, I had seen the man in Beirut struggling for his life, and I did not comprehend that I had not immediately recognised in him my father.

Only I caught myself and asked my brother to continue.

It had then become more propitious again, had seized him in the chest sometimes, had flown tumbling about his head, but it would not have confused him and his attendant any further, except that the habitually hard, rough man had been muted by a strange meekness and indulgence.

Until that morning towards eleven when death had entered the room unexpectedly.

The now pale man had taken in with good appetite a small breakfast consisting of an egg and a mug of broth, and had sunk back unhurriedly into a daydream on the sofa. Then he started suddenly and asked the housekeeper to look out at who was going past on the street below. The old woman, who did not hear any wagon's rattle, nevertheless stepped to the window so as to not irritate him, but found the street to be empty and quiet and disabused him sparingly of his error. But then he rose energetically, went to her, looked down and asked stricken, what had stolen the eyes from her head? Down below a wagon from Tannhausen was travelling past. But what was that about and why had it stopped below as well, since he was not at all in a state for making a journey. Shaking his head, he headed to his place shaken. But when he arrived at the table, his knees jerked as though by a soundless blow. The woman realised who had touched him, grabbed for him and screamed out shrilly at the same time. Then the already completely smitten man turned his head up once more and said with gently reproving voice, 'Why are you screaming? You see I'm going to heaven." Then he tried to laugh, only it turned into the short, rattling sound of death. My brother was seized more by the enigmatic circumstances of this separation than by the death itself, which isn't appalling with an old man of seventy eight years. For, if the presentiment of death really travelled invisibly next to us the whole time through life, you would in fact not be permitted to have a peaceful hour anymore.

I saw how good it had been that I had kept silent about my experience. With that he went and I accompanied him to the front door. Then I turned back in order to be alone for a while in the room to think over the strange affairs. My family had never possessed a member who had walked with their head in the clouds so to speak. The world ran soberly through all their eyes.

Thinking thus, I went back down the corridor and opened the door to the living room. But, there I would very soon be a little frightened. Next to an old glass cabinet, there was a leather covered armchair in which my father tended to have his midday nap and quiet rests. As I now stood on the threshold, I saw my father incarnate sitting in his old place and looking up with a stricken face, as if he wanted to ask me what curious thing had occurred that I had to enter unexpectedly and disturb him in his slumber.

In that moment, I was so confused that I was on the point of answering. But then a breath snatched the image into the ether.

After the burial, I travelled to Berlin. At the time, the acquisition of Jiaozhou lay in the air for insiders, and I had been asked as connoisseur of the East to a lecture in the Colonial Office. Glad to be snatched from this ghostly circle, I went there and delivered my expert opinion. Then I spent a few extremely animated days in the company of scholarly and unscholarly friends. Only, a shadow lay in my soul which nothing could dissipate. As soon as I was alone, a melancholy befell me, a sorrow which dully tormented me that it wasn't going well for my father after his death and that he was dwelling in a place which wasn't good. How easy the Japanese, Chinese and Catholics have it vis-a-vis such intangible afflictions. For me, the Westerner and Protestant, the protective wall against the universe had been suddenly pulled away. I wandered as though by an abyss and threw as it were a shadow onto the other side. To no avail, I began a restless journey through Germany, in vain I delved into scientific work. My receptiveness and my productivity were inexhaustible. Only, when it turned towards evening, whether I was alone or in company, it was all the same. My world stretched into the immeasurable, and a dejectedness attacked me, as if I stood in the midst of an endless dreary desert which led all around into invisible chambers of soundless torments, and I often asked myself sorrowfully without knowing it, 'Where could my father be?'

My condition worsened so much that a friendly professor of neurology became alert to it: for I had sunk down in company one evening with eyes lost to it, murmuring to myself and beginning to speak. He tapped me on the shoulder earnestly on parting and requested imperatively that I visit him the following morning.

Instead I packed my bags in the hotel immediately after arriving and travelled in that same night over the Alps to Italy.

The next night, I was already sleeping in Portofino Kulm above Santa Margherita. —

You have surely also experienced it, I believe there are no men at all whose lives have been spared this nervous surprise: of course, a certain emotional disposition belongs with it, which however can be different in every case. You stand in absolutely quiet solitude and listen to the only

sound to be heard, the beating of your own heart.
As you lose yourself in the pounding of this
mysterious clock, you believe you hear it around
you, sometimes here, sometimes there outside
your body, and not long after our heartbeat
seems to have completely deserted us and have
wandered into the world. The tree pulses with it,
the mountains convulses with its ghostly quiet
thundering, we hear it pounding in the water,
and even the sky trembles rhythmically under its
pounding: only we ourselves, we from whom it
originates, we are shut out from it and
experience something like the torment of a dead
man who has kept a consciousness of his death,
or of a living man whose feel for death is his only
sense of life.

My spiritual state was thereabouts, gentlemen, above all because I lay in waiting, as if with
a thousand eyes around me, for that which
eluded my comprehension.

Now I know exactly the therapy which my
dear neurologist would have used against this
suffering, purely external means, all the calming
which I had prescribed myself in those months
systematised and, in a somewhat motley manner,
used. Since we must hear our foolishness first as
well-considered insight from the mouth of
another in order to recognise its inanity, it
straightaway became clear to me by the
professor's earnestness that I was seeking on an

entirely wrong path to escape the shadows from my father's grave which were troubling me. That's why I had fled, to free myself according to my own system from the afflictions of my shattered gaze. I wanted to stop attempting to mow clouds with the scythe and deal with this internal affair internally as well. Fanciful images from the imagination which ambush us in the dark are robbed of their unpleasantness, not when you flee before them, but when you make towards them and expose them with fearless eyes.

I wanted to accomplish that in Portofino Kulm. For the whole rational mastery of the Westerner had seized me from behind again, and I was charged with impatience to go behind the shadowboxing of my soul.

The hotel in which I lodged lay supine, connected by the Portofino peninsula with the foothills of the Apennines, and consisted at the time only of a quiet house, which has now unfortunately been degraded by the attachment of a stupid, puffed-up temple to food. Constantly beset by the feeling of a double-life which was constantly disturbed by subconscious currents in the certainty of its mundane present, this place seemed made for me. A place where you look over the sea from two sides and hear sometimes from Camogli, sometimes from Santa Marghe-rita, the whistle of the locomotive with which the train plunges itself into the tunnel which undermines the ridge. The ghostly state of my soul should thus be led in the simplest way into the facts of external circumstances and thereby made better. You see, gentlemen, I wasn't entirely the naive, superstitious victim of a sort of madness.

It was between autumn and summer, the Italians, seeking cooler climes, already gone, the Germans still there. Excepting myself, only an elderly couple from Saxony were resident in the house. As is my custom, I filled up the morning with serious work, the afternoon with patrolling the environment, and the only resource of spiritual diet that I prescribed myself consisted of the complete liberation of my spirit from the feeling of an obstruction or flight. I assuaged myself and floated in the light over the blue sea, in the restful sound of the tree tops, in the violet glow with which the Apennines hovered on many evenings like a wreath of fanciful, giant, amazing flowers in the high air.

But I would experience that the fulfillment of my hopes would surprise me in a different way to that I chose. For nobody could have thought of such a solution.

When I climbed up the steep ravine from the Dorian tombs in San Fruttuoso late one afternoon, I heard someone behind me walking the same path, turned around, called, waited at a bend in the path for the man to finally catch up to me, but caught sight of nobody, felt however, as I rested a little on a stone, that someone was sitting next to me. Not bearing down, not heavy, no, a quiet, comforting being.

I knew at the time, and as well as anyone today, about the phenomenon of the splitting of the personality, by which such bewilderingly confused things are offered to us in dreaming, and took this invisible being next to me for nothing other than the reflection of my personality and, indeed, that calm, satisfied part which had collected itself again to its old strength in the godlike peace of this magnificent corner of earth. Pondering further the strange, marvellous swirling of our inner worlds, I rose, got the better of the last ascent and stepped through the natural gate formed by stones shunted together and off the tended path which wound in an easy rhythm of gentle rising and falling around the little summits which dress the mountain chain.

While I was strolling so sedately under the greenery of the elms' waving branches, sometimes supping with delighted looks on the beauty of the basin in which the village of Ruta's vineyards climbed down in drifts towards Santa Margherita, sometimes looking out as a pleasant distraction at the colourful cliffs which draw towards Genoa, I carried on a dreamy dialogue with the being which had found me on the path up to San Fruttuoso. Our thinking is of course mostly a speaking in thoughts. Only in moments of inner flowing apart or extreme stress is it a play of inconceivable knowing which creates and obliterates its incomprehensible developments behinds the facts of life. Nothing other than comparable to a light, it wavers in me and adheres to my side at the same time.

Oh, gentlemen, this little while on the rising and falling little path around Portofino Kulm gave me a marvellous, precious feeling of being bound by my inner being to all the universe's inner being, beyond all the bonds of earth and life.

At a turn in the path, it suddenly broke off. It seemed to me as though I expired. It went through me like a jolt and I could only keep to myself by closing my eyes. When I opened them, I was alone again. I had locked together with myself, not the same self which had just felt pleasant and happy as though poured out into all the world around me, but I had locked together anew with the being which had strayed for weeks burdened and fearful through Germany and fled here. The old deterioration juddered through me again.

Next to me, placed in a narrow strip of meadow, an arbour-like frame made of posts struck together rose up, and on the wooden benches running around its inside, Italian farmers were sitting with wife and child before their glasses, which were filled with dark red wine. They were eating white bread with it and raising a considerable, lighthearted noise.

While I watched, I felt a darkness and pallor in my face. The men immediately fell silent before me, the strangely sinister man, and the women looked at me full of pity.

"*Bona sera, Signore,*" the farmers murmured and raised their crushed hats reverently.

Then I pulled myself together from my disarray, replied to their greeting with forced laughter and then strove hurriedly to my apartment.

Around the Apennines, a grey smoke was falling from the blind heavens, below to the left and right, the sea lay discoloured and restive, and white snakes of foam began to run at the the cliffs. Only around Genoa was there still a piercing, yellow light. The city looked like a giant galleon on the point of pushing off from land and making at top speed for the open sea to save itself from the storm which was brewing. 'Yes, but it won't be so quick with the wind here,' I thought in quickly striding on and looked up searchingly again. Everything grey on grey. The whole sky. Only in one place, as though with an untoward, great blast, had a hole been ripped in the wall of clouds so that you could see into the bowels of the universe. Indeed, it looked like a burning, gangrenous wound. And now, as I watched more closely in astonishment, a little white cloud, a soft, hazy veil, swung up, wavered dallying by the smoking red wound and glided delicately in to the chasm, but without being streaked by its fervour either. White, pristine, the little cloud lost itself in the depths, and I observed with incredulous astonishment that as the little veil advanced further, the sky began to glow green at the base of the crack, as if it was burnished by the reflection of the meadows of paradise.

'But it's all no use,' I pondered, feeling nothing of the foolishness of my sentiment, but rather still comforted in a grim schadenfreude, because I was connecting the appearance and disappearance of the little white cloud with the glimmering light which had pursued me as though from the other side of the world in vain. At the same time, I felt the lack of worth of my spiritual state, stormed ahead and, now running more than walking, arrived past the man-servant, who, indolent and lazy, leant on the wall next to the door of the hotel, and went to my room.

There I threw myself into an armchair in abandonment, shattered, dulled, and was in no state to collect myself for a long time. Finally the incomprehensible agitation transformed into the melancholic, comfortless torpidity which had burdened me constantly since the death of my father.

The entire house was still as night, full of the desolation of uninhabited spaces. Two rooms along from me, I heard through the thin walls the aged, vibrating, humming crooning of a woman's voice ringing out. 'Oh only once in my entire life", an old, sentimental song. It was probably the previously mentioned wife of the old Saxon singing. It sounded to me like the helpless sound of fear, and it seemed to have got completely past my restraint. I bent down to the window, took my head in both my hands, and struggling against tears, I murmured, 'Where could my father be?' And with that I felt full of a steady, glassy clarity, my senses awoke raptly in an indescribable transparency.

At this moment, I heard the soft, dull grumble of a gently moved, large door. Firm, manly steps walked down the hall and climbed the stairs up to the corridor off which my room lay. At first I thought it was the man-servant who, his idle dreaming by the wall at an end, was going to work again. But the rhythm of the steps, the manner in which the feet were set down decisively, seemed familiar to me. I sat up in the armchair and listened as the gait on the carpet of the unknown person neared unhesitatingly and paused in front of my room for a moment. Then I saw how the door handle was lightly pressed down. The door opened a crack, and my father, my father incarnate, stretched his head inside. His face was cheerful and bore the traits of roguishness, as I had been used to see with my father from my early youth, the sunny days of our well-being, when his being blossomed in joy. He looked at me thus with a long deep glance, nodded to me encouragingly and attentively, and disappeared.

I had not been tempted by a breath of my soul to ask a question. Everything had happened with wondrous matter-of-factness. Every burden on my nature, every sorrow over my father's fate, every melancholy which had seized me over the final hopelessness of all life had been blown away like dust. My father, he appeared well kept to me, and I myself had the feeling that my existence in all my future would flow more surely.

With a deep, liberated breath, I rose from my seat at the window, leant my forehead on the pane and gazed in happy excitement at the Ligurian Sea and the colourful coast below, where, at Nervi, Bogliasco and Recco, a last, evening light was being painted, easing itself from the land before Genoa, wandering out into the sea slowly and despondently and sinking there into the dull waters.

Since that evening, gentlemen, I don't ask myself anymore about the meaning of life. The world is illuminated deeper to me from outside my life, and I don't feel guided by my will alone anymore.

I am certain that my comprehension does not come from knowing and that the happiness of mankind has nothing to do with well-being and success, but only exists in becoming one with that nameless power which forms the deepest part of our being, and before time and space together, my ego and everything else are nothing but circles on a pond."

When Florian Brustat had concluded, the listeners, the judge, Wiese, the school principal, Leutner, and the mayor, Musiol, sat silently and absorbed for a long time.

They did not dare to look over at the researcher, who had come a little way away with his chair in the intense narration of the conclusion of his mysterious experience and was sitting almost in the middle of the path which led to the lawn on which the table stood. The vault of the late night sky was not visible. Shapeless, heavy darkness lay around everything and over them, and the three men looked up astonished into this dreary blackness as if they held it possible that some shimmer would penetrate through or creep over, which was the effect of those depths which the researcher's tale had just opened to them.

Then, as though after quiet agreement, the company rose, moved wordlessly towards the gate and disbanded in silence.

The mine shafts around about were snoring, high in the air there was a humming like the cautious flight of brazen flocks of birds, and the hauling engines clattered like the hooves of trotting horses being driven on a hard road and making no headway. But it was all being blown away by the spirit-breaths of midnight.

About the Publisher

Our mission is to provide translations into English of the complete works of neglected major European writers. We do not cherry-pick works that seem the most marketable, but rather seek to provide a complete collection of each writer's works so that readers can follow the writer's development and decide on its merits for themselves.

http://www.facebook.com/KANitzPublishing